I0713864

Things You Cannot Say With Your Mouth

Carnelian Heart Short Story Anthology 2024

First published in Great Britain in 2024 by:

Carnelian Heart Publishing Ltd
Suite A
82 James Carter Road
Mildenhall
Suffolk
IP28 7DE
UK

www.carnelianheartpublishing.co.uk

©Each individual story, the contributing author
©This anthology as a collective work, Carnelian Heart Publishing Ltd 2024

Paperback ISBN   978-1-914287-91-6
Hardback ISBN   978-1-914287-92-3
Ebook ISBN   978-1-914287-93-0

A catalogue record for this book is available from the British Library.

All rights reserved. No part of this publication may be reproduced, stored in a retrieval system or transmitted in any form or by any means, electronic, mechanical, photocopying, recording or otherwise without prior written permission from the publisher.

Edited by Lazarus Panashe Nyagwambo
Proofread by Samantha Rumbidzai Vazhure

Cover art:
Paperback – Tatenda Thumba
Hardback – 'Silence' (2024), by Samantha Rumbidzai Vazhure

Cover layout:
Mike Stuart

Internal design:
Typeset by Carnelian Heart Publishing Ltd
Layout and formatting by DanTs Media

Table of Contents

Foreword

The Carnelian Heart Short Story Anthology 2024 is a collection of stories by African writers selected from the short story competition organised by Carnelian Heart Publishing as part of their vision to bring the richness of African writing to a global stage and provide opportunities for African writers, both established and new, who are trying to set their mark in the literary world.

The 2024 edition had over a hundred submissions from authors all over Africa, of which 19 were shortlisted for publication in this anthology, a roster which includes authors from Zimbabwe, Nigeria, South Africa, Kenya and Egypt. Three winning stories were selected from the nineteen and their authors awarded different cash prizes and publishing contracts.

The winners of the 2024 competition were:

1. 'The Cafeteria' by Tanaka Chidora
2. 'All is Fair' by Victor Ajwang
3. 'God Created A Thing' by Fatima Okhuosami

The final stories were compiled and edited by Lazarus Panashe Nyagwambo.

The titular story, 'Things you cannot say with your mouth', was written by Joseph Jegede

Congratulations to all the finalists!

~Samantha Rumbidzai Vazhure, Founding Editor - Carnelian Heart Publishing Ltd.

"When all else fails, don't take it in silence: scream like hell, scream like Jericho was tumbling down, serenaded by a brace of trombones, scream"

~Dambudzo Marechera

Tanaka Chidora

Tanaka Chidora is a writer, literary critic, and academic based at the University of Malawi, in the Department of Literary Studies, where he teaches Creative Writing, African Literature, and Theories of Literature. He is the author of BECAUSE SADNESS IS BEAUTIFUL?, a collection of poems published in 2019. He has also published short stories and poems in various anthologies. Recently, he did a commissioned translation of Tsitsi Dangarembga's THE BOOK OF NOT into Shona. The manuscript of his debut novel, CARRYING A COUNTRY IN YOUR FOREHEAD, was longlisted for the Iland Prize (2023). The novel will, hopefully, be published in 2024.

The Cafeteria
Tanaka Chidora – Zimbabwe

Sickness can travel in the air, all the way from the hospital beds to the cafeteria, and you can smell it in the food you buy, taste it on your tongue, and feel it slither down your oesophagus with the rice and chicken and the beverage you could have bought to accompany the food. It can make you hate hospital cafeteria food, especially on the first day when you go seeking to have a sick relative admitted. The smell of sickness and the medicines that are used to fight sickness, and the sight of sick people and their relatives who seem to be pleading with sickness to have mercy, can all put you off hospital cafeteria food.

"Doctors and nurses are on strike," you could be told on the first day. "We'll admit your relative and hope the nurses and doctors will come back any time from now."

On the first day, in the evening, sickness can go home with you. You could be someone who is not used to sickness's companionship, so you can try to lose sickness in the crowd. But when there are no nurses and doctors, sickness can be cleverer than you and cannot be lost in a crowd. It can catch up with you as you stand in a winding queue for the government bus and can look at you with those accusing eyes that seem to be asking, since when have you become this ill-mannered?

By the third day, by the time you realise that the doctors and nurses are damn serious, and no one is going to do a thing about it, and the strike is going to continue indefinitely, sickness could have become a ubiquitous presence in your life. It can stay inside your tummy even after you go home, and can appear on TV while you are trying to watch the president deliver a State of the Nation Address (affectionately abbreviated SONA by the TV anchor), accompany you to your bed and sleep between you and your partner, banish love-making to reminiscences of that period before untreated sickness happened, and invade your dream with a whip to chase out all frivolous actors who have the audacity to come into a dream at a time when untreated sickness is the only thing that matters…

When doctors and nurses strike and sickness is left untreated, it can eat your breakfast, or, if its generosity is at a likeable level, eat with you, its smell creeping into your nostrils and reminding you that there is an old man lying on a creaky hospital bed, an old man with ribs that look like the collapsing roof of an old hut, an old man whose crime is to be born at a time when the cost of dying is the same as that of living. Sickness can go out of the house with you in the morning, walk by your side along the dusty footpath that leads to the local township where sun-weary travellers with sweating bodies push, scratch and squeeze their way into a rattling government bus, eager to outwit each other into the only cheap bus that comes once a day. Sickness can be patient, too, and can afford to wait with you for an illegal Toyota FunCargo taxi if you happen to fail to outwit other sun-weary passengers into the government bus. Sickness can walk about in the sun with you, gazing listlessly at ghetto youth sitting under the rust-eaten roof of the collapsing bus terminus which no passenger uses anymore; ghetto youth holding crochets and interpreting patterns on each other's heads, ganja spliffs hanging on the corners of their mouths like lizards trying to catch the last rays of a disappearing sun from the crevices of an exfoliating layer of a rock's dome.

When a Toyota FunCargo finally comes, sickness can squeeze its way between you and the passenger who chooses to sit with his legs acres apart, eating into the space of two more people right there at the back of the Toyota FunCargo, until a tout tells the passenger to stop sitting carelessly as if they own the car. "If you want to sit like that, buy your own car," the tout can ridicule the selfish passenger. Sickness can agree with you that that's not how you sit in a Toyota FuCargo taxi that does not belong to you.

When sickness has been around for some time, with all the nurses and doctors on strike, it can know you the way your shadow knows you. It can know what you like and what you do not like. It can know the indifference with which you enter through the hospital gate as you visit your sick relative at 12:30 p.m. or 5:30 p.m., faithfully holding a bundle of bananas whose yellow is transitioning towards a wet brown, or apples with soft sides that feel as tender as fontanelle, sides that you fear to press with your fingers because they may burst under their weight. When doctors and nurses strike, sickness can become the guard who stands at the hospital gate because guards rarely strike. Sickness can become the chap with a pushcart selling apples and bananas, or the woman sitting in the red soil, leaning against the collapsing hospital fence, selling *maputi* and *freezits* to tired hospital visitors. When doctors and nurses go on strike, sickness can enter the hospital gate with you and walk about aimlessly with you as you dread getting inside to an unchanged world.

Sickness, like your shadow, can go with you into the hospital waiting area teeming with people who, like you, are there with their sick relatives because they cannot keep them at home. Keeping a sick relative at home is like wishing them dead. Even your neighbours can start suspecting you of being a witch or a member of the get-rich-quick brigade who can kill their relatives for bundles of money. Sickness can stand with you right there in the outpatient area as you dread going to the ward where your relative was admitted a day before (or on the day of) the strike, two weeks back, and where he could be remaining because there is no one to attend to him or to discharge him.

In the first days, the sight of frail bodies can make you cringe like someone walking on a rocky path littered with millipedes after a drizzle. The food at the cafeteria can smell of sickness and you can only eat a little before choosing to fish out a portable whisky flask. You can take some swigs to banish sickness's peeping form and complain to another visitor about the poor standards of hospital cafeteria food. The visitor, who could be eating rice and sausages, can stare at you briefly before grunting and continuing with his eating. You can sit there at the cafeteria until visiting hour. You know there will be no change, but you can visit anyway.

***

Sometimes, after the 12 p.m. visit, and after many days of sickness's loyal companionship, you can decide to walk to the city to sit in the park, or to walk into Twilight Sports Bar and buy a Black Label quart and watch Liverpool play Man U. Between the park and Twilight Sports Bar, you can choose Twilight Sports Bar. You can either go on an empty stomach or eat sadza and chicken and soup at the hospital cafeteria.

After eating, you can walk to the city, but if the game is about to begin, you can catch an illegal Honda Fit or FunCargo taxi that can leave you at Corner Leopold and Samora. Whichever choice you make, sickness can make it too, so you two are inseparable. You can even share the Black Label quart and support the same team. You could be at that stage where you are no longer wary of sickness's ashen and cracked, sometimes bleeding, lips. When sickness has been your companion for a long time, you can no longer see certain things. If Liverpool scores, you can slap sickness's shoulders in excitement. If Man U scores, sickness can look at you mockingly and burst into laughter.

It could be that you have become very close friends now.

***

One day in the morning, your partner can ask you what you want to eat for breakfast. You can tell her that you can grab something in OK Supermarket on your way to work. But because of the urgency of getting to work to complete your tasks before the 12:30 p.m. hospital visit, you can forget to buy food in OK supermarket. At 1 p.m., you can rush out of your workplace and flag down a commuter omnibus. By the time you reach the hospital, it could be 1:37 p.m. You can rush to the ward where your relative is and find a few relatives scattered around the bed of the sick relative whose active eyes betray the disintegration of a body that, only three months back, could have been energetic and alive.

After the visit, you can gather outside and talk about the sick relative, how he actually drank a whole bottle of *Pfuko maheu* and nibbled at an apple. He is improving, a relative can say, and all of you can agree with the relative, although deep down, nagging reservations about the relative's observation can send ominous ripples to your heads. Before going back to work, you can go the hospital cafeteria to grab a quick lunch. The food can surprise you, and even though sickness could be sitting by your side as you are eating, you can still afford to let your tongue savour the watery soup. You can even chew the tender chicken bones until the marrow and the fragments of the bones become one inseparable thing that you can swallow.

You can now start to look forward to hospital cafeteria food.

***

One morning, on your way to work, you can decide to pass by the hospital. It could be that you know relatives cannot visit at that hour, but you know you can sweet-talk one of the receptionists to allow you to see your relative. You can arrive at the receptionist with a smile and tell them that you are so-and-so's benefactor. The receptionist can wave you through. You can go up the stairs with an elevator, but the elevator could be out of service – not an unusual phenomenon. When you get to your relative's bed, you can find a strange face there, and you can go down to the receptionist to inform them that you found a strange face on your relative's hospital bed. The receptionist can scrutinise your face, recognition slowly dawning in his eyes the way western boulders slowly unveil their crowns in sync with the sun's lackadaisical emergence in the east.

"Wait here," the receptionist can say before disappearing through a door, appearing a few seconds later with a forced smile, that kind of smile that one can put on to hide an evil deed.

"Our counsellor is coming to speak to you."

***

You can take your phone from your pocket and dial the number of your partner or her mother to tell them that the sick relative is no more, or you can wait a little bit, think deeply about how to handle the situation. Breaking such news can be a headache. You can choose to think deeply about how to proceed while eating something at the hospital cafeteria. In fact, it could be that you are probably missing the smell of the rice and chicken relish that you could have become accustomed to at the hospital cafeteria.

You can eat slowly, savouring the taste that could have become a part of you since the sick relative was admitted here three weeks back. After eating, you can buy a coke and drink it unhurriedly, dreading the phone call at the end of which a wail could rent the already rent morning air of Magamba Hostels where touts, vendors, thieves and local ward politicians are milling about, each marking their territory in the crowded spaces of a dying city. A city can die even with people in it. A country too.

***

Eight weeks after the burial of the relative, roughly eleven days after Christmas, you can abruptly rise from your creaking office chair which could have stopped swivelling way before you had inherited the office from a retiring professor. You can stand at the window, gazing outside at the lazy trickle of students who are moving about. It is one of those months of dry spells, so the lethargic sky above could be sadistically holding a blazing sun to a wilting earth the way a sadistic boy casts the reflection of the sun to unsuspecting cyclists. You could be missing a cigarette, but your worsening hay fever could have given you a final notice.

Maybe lunch at the hospital cafeteria, you can think to yourself. The idea can brighten your day, and just like that, you can bang the door behind you and rush to the *kombi* terminus.

***

The rice and chicken can stare at you listlessly, exciting no excitement. A chicken wing could be submerged in the soup, only a piece of it floating on top like the smallest tip of the fin of a shark that is disappearing into the depths of an ocean a distance from where you could be standing. The smell of sickness can be present too, giving to eating the unwanted feeling of slurping at the slimy entrails of sickness itself.

16

Victor Ajwang

Victor Ajwang is a Kenyan lawyer, writer and film enthusiast. His micro-films *Dreams from Congo* and *Being a Child* have won awards at the Moinho Cine Fest and Sabira Cole Film Festival respectively. When he is not binge watching movies or working on briefs, he writes prose fiction. He lives in Nairobi with his Family.

You can follow him on X (formerly Twitter) @AJVeec or Linkedin @vajwang

All Is Fair

Victor Ajwang – Kenya

The soldier gunned a rusty old HSV hard along the hills of Kabizo, oblivious of the blood soaking through his Man's Field. Even though it was noon and the sun hung low, his uniform was drenched in water, and the wind chill made it feel as though he was riding over the peaks of an icy mountain. It did not seem to bother him. His eyes were pricked on the copperhead-coloured murram slithering beneath him at sixty-five miles an hour, his instincts sharper than surgical blades. His thoughts, however, were a ways off…

He wondered what he would tell the boss. That a soldier would, in such times when young, able men were more elusive than the diamonds of Tshikapa, steal a fellow comrade's life… it was unheard of. General Nkunda was a commander made of steel, whose law came second to none but the Lord's own divine edict. And he was just as unchanging. He ruled his men with an iron fist and had no patience for weakness. Judgement would be certain and swift: death by hanging. There was no excuse for it. He yanked the throttle; the motorcycle whined and called for another gear, but every last horsepower was in use and there was none to give.

Only two weeks ago, the militia had rummaged through Kivu, conscripting anyone with a male name who could lift a MAS-49. Mothers who protested were slapped around; the leaner ones taken behind bushes and their husbands made to watch impotently. And if a man shed a tear, he got lynched faster than a Tutsi in Kinshasa. Those foolish enough to resist found themselves dumped in marshes along unnamed footpaths, to be forgotten as quickly as their heroics. By order of General Nkunda. Naturally, a third of the new recruits were thinned out on the march back to camp. Physical weakness, disease… nostalgia; reasons for thinning were not in short supply. A well-placed slug to the temple made quick work of it. It seemed cruel, but the militia had higher-ups to answer to, objectives to achieve, areas of land to clear, stubborn civilians to scare off. They had no apologies.

All that pressure, yet *he* had gone and killed General Nkunda's best and only sniper, arguably the most crucial asset in the General's war chest. He would be disciplined. There was no doubt about it – nay, *he would be punished*. Yet his grip on the throttle tightened with each kilometre the motorcycle ate up, ever moving closer to his destiny. Perhaps he wanted to die.

But what about the girl? Was it right, what he had done?

He had met her on the banks of a tropical river, under a sky droning with helicopters and a barrage of rockets. She had just finished bathing, and the offensive took her by surprise. She was moderately slender and wore a long muslin dress from under which a voluptuous body made curvatures here and there, revealing just enough to ignite a furious longing in him. Her dark chocolate complexion created a sublime counterpoint to bright, hazel eyes and long lashes. Her hair was plaited in five neat rows, whose ends were tied together in a flowing strand. He thought she had an unusually small nose. Yet, through all those soft edges, an obstinate, intelligent determination radiated from within, culminating in the most intense look the soldier recalled ever having encountered.

"I don't need your protection," she had said with a defiant look, "what I need – *what we all need* – is for you soldiers to leave our villages alone! We are tired and exhausted. You have broken us a hundred times over. Is it not enough? When will it be enough?"

"You don't understand," he had said quietly.

"You will rape and kill me if I don't move, is that it?"

"You are in danger. There is a battalion of soldiers coming this way, and they will do much worse than that. Trust me." She had expected a violent outburst, and his momentary gentility disarmed her. If only for a moment.

That was ages ago. He was a soldier. She was a gloomy girl on the banks of a tropical river. And it was more than enough. They snuck around whenever his unit was posted near her village. He knew all actively patrolled areas, and in that way, managed to avoid running into fellow soldiers. Even when she confessed, months later, of having been an informer for the army in another life, the soldier still found himself confoundingly in need of her camaraderie. He assured himself she was only a girl and could not pose any credible danger to the militia. Somewhere within him, he knew the real reasons were far more irrational.

She told him of a younger girl. One who used to go on adventures high in the mountains. A girl who had a quirky laugh and could run faster than all the boys in Virunga. She had wild dreams and unfathomable ends, the girl she spoke of. She was hopeful and full of youth, maybe even a little naïve. But then, she would grow. She would witness things, *go through things*, and by the time past met present, the one would become the other, and the gloom would return like a ceaseless storm cloud.

He, feeling obliged to reciprocate, told her of a boy who fell in love with theatre in the streets of Kindu, who had an everlasting smile that could not fade, and laughed and lived and seized every moment without a care for what tomorrow had to say about it. He wanted to be a stage performer. That is, until his mother died, and rumours began spreading that he was the seed of a brigand who did unspeakable things with the FDLR. Somewhere along the way, the boy lost his smile and a soldier emerged in his stead.

They swam in the tropical river and ate wild fruits, and for a time, began entertaining odd ideas. For example, that the world in which those two children had lived was not lost but was hidden from sight by some evil *ndoki*. That they could find a *nganga* to bring it back. Or at least reveal it to them. There, they imagined, they would find the two children.

On a sunny, blissful day under the gentle caress of a zephyr and the ethereal, minty scent of a chaste tree growing nearby, she touched his hand. Across wispy blades of grass, a silent message passed between them, and they drew close. Her breath was heaven…

Presently, the camp's watchtowers (two wooden boxes on stilts) shot up from the horizon as soldier and motorcycle closed in. The soldier turned a gear and pulled on the throttle hard enough to blister his fingers. His uniform was beginning to dry up. The question returned to his mind again. What would he tell the boss? He could not simply blurt about the approaching FARDC battalion; General Nkunda would be curious as to what he had been doing in Kwala in the first place, and that might very well lead to the girl's discovery.

All is fair in love and war, he told himself. He had learned the phrase back in Kindu while performing a homemade recitation of Shakespeare's *Henry V*. The question could not be ignored; *what would he tell the boss?*

What would he tell the boss? What would he tell– in an instant, the front wheel violently twisted back into the motorcycle and the whole contraption leapt into the air. A second of distraction was all it took. The two incompatible masses, metal and flesh, turned on their heads and began to fall.

For two weeks now, she had insisted on meeting him. *He needed time to arrange a safe place on a safe day*, he had told her. Unconfirmed reports had been coming in that FARDC was planning a major operation in the area. There was a flurry of unplanned, half-organized activity, which made keeping track of movement patterns quite difficult. Still, she insisted on meeting him. She said it was important. She said she had no choice. And so, they quickly arranged to meet somewhere along the banks of the tropical river on that day. General Nkunda had given him the motorcycle as reward for leading a successful raid in the belly of Mahondo. He took it and went to the river while his unit was on foot patrol outside the camp.

He found the girl looking off in the distance, as though she had lost sight of a homebound aircraft. She jumped when she heard his footsteps and looked troubled.

"Are you okay? What is it?" he asked. The spark of defiance in her eyes was gone, replaced by a lingering something. What it was, he could not finger. "What is it?" he repeated, getting anxious.

She spoke fearfully. "We need to run, Tuti, the army is coming!" He was slow and did not immediately think to inquire as to how she had come about that knowledge. She continued frantically. "I have accepted my place, but please don't let the militia take him. Don't let any of them take him!"

"Take who, what are you talking about?"

She began breaking down right there, and a thorn pricked something deep inside of him.

What feeling was that?

He made as if to embrace her but froze; a strange man, not much older than himself, had appeared from nowhere.

Oblivious of it, the soldier had grown a 'tail' on his way to the river. The brigand's name was Tukio, and he was known in the whole of Kivu, from Tate to Watamu: General Nkunda's best sniper. He had twenty confirmed kills under his clip, all Congolese, a triumph he wore like a silver badge of the Légion d'honneur. His face was nearly as ugly as the malice in his only eye; a battle scar ran the length of it on one side, momentarily ceasing over the dead, shrivelled hole that was supposed to house the second eye; papules and blackheads blotched his face; and he had a circular stump of dried skin on his forehead like the residual patch of a disbudded horn. In a word, he was a hideous freak of nature. He looked between the two, reading the situation, and finally settled on the girl, eyes burning with bestial hunger distilled in a furnace of pure malice.

"What do we have here," said ugly face, yellowed teeth grinning at the paralysed prey. "I see you have found yourself *kwanga* while the rest of us starve, *eh?* You are dangerous, my guy!" A mirthful grin was sent in the soldier's direction. "What do you say, comrade, shall we share a meal?"

The soldier was first paralysed. Then something came over him, and he lunged. One second, he was glaring at Tukio with flaming eyes, the next they were rolling down the banks into the river. The two bodies became one brawling mess in the splash and spill of the ensuing struggle. The soldier felt something sharp stab his belly. He lost his footing and fell back in the river.

Tukio staggered up, his ugly face still grinning murderously.

Then a shot rang off, and it was all over.

Tukio fell to his knees and collapsed.

As the dead body floated by, their blood mixed and carried off with the water in a translucent cloud of crimson.

A bad omen.

The soldier staggered to his feet. He looked between the girl holding Tukio's riffle and the floating corpse, and suddenly felt afraid. More afraid than he had ever felt his entire life. He saw General Nkunda's choleric face towering above him, flames of lava for eyes, nostrils breathing out boiling steam, passing judgement upon him and casting him to the bottomless pit of hell. Fear gave way to frustration, frustration gave way to anger, anger to indignation, and the last was cast upon the girl.

"This is all your fault!" he bawled, approaching her.

"No," she pleaded, "listen to me, we can get away from all this, just like we—"

"Have you been spying on us for the army?"

"What? No!"

"Why did it have to be today!?"

"The army have this position surrounded, Tuti. I can get us safe pass—"

Before she could finish the sentence, he pounced on her, wrapping his fingers tightly around her throat. "Look what you did! I will be executed. All because of you!"

Through a collapsing windpipe, she managed to say, "I... am... pregnant." The news came out of left field and knocked him back. His fingers eased but he did not let go. Heaving, she quickly added "I am pregnant with your—" cough "—child!"

He froze, fear rising in his spine again.

Eyes darted, searching.

Searching for the slightest hint that it wasn't true.

That she was just saying it to save herself.

There was none.

His heart sank.

It was often said that evil men were sometimes cursed to repeat their lives over and over again without end. He thought of his father, the brigand. He thought of himself, no soldier, just another brigand. He looked at those begging, petrified eyes.

Could he really let another outlaw into this wretched world?

Why torture the damned thing with life at all?

His fingers began tightening again.

"You could have run!" he cried through clenched teeth and a torrent of silent tears. "You could have run away and never come back! Why did you stay?"

She pleaded, and fought, and scratched, and flailed, and finally, sagged.

When the deed was done, he fell back in the dirt and looked around at the totality of his miserable existence, sobbing quietly. For the first time in a very long time, the brigand's loneliness felt total and absolute. He stared at the girl's still body for what felt like hours. Then, like the whisper of an enchantress calling him out of a dream, he heard commotion over the forest. Then louder commotion. Then even louder commotion. He looked at the dead girl.

There was little doubt about it. Still trembling, he jumped on his motorcycle and gunned his way out of the forest; the militia had to be warned…

Presently, he staggered up in a daze. The crash was bad, and he thought he heard something inside him break with the crunch of a dry twig. His wound had gotten worse since the river. Fortunately, adrenaline was blocking everything; the avalanche would come later. A quick cost-benefit analysis of the carnage made it apparent he would have to go the rest of the way on foot. And so he did.

"General Nkunda. I have to speak to General Nkunda," he told the children with AKs outside the General's quarters when he finally made camp. They eyed him suspiciously, his blood-soaked garment a seemingly minor detail.

"What for?" inquired the smallest among them, scratching an invisible stubble, his chin tilted up at a spot in the sky as if a strike drone might emerge at any moment.

"We are getting attacked. Open the door, *now*."

After a minute more of inquiry and suspicious glances, the largest among them led him into the General's chambers, a converted house that belonged to a dead physician.

The General, as it turned out, was a disreputable-looking man of medium height and a moderately built frame. He was shabbily dressed in a tatty camouflage suit that may have once been green, but which had faded to a brittle brown with time and hardship. His uniform was matched with worn leather shoes that could not have accounted for much other than keeping his feet off the ground. His sense of style was replicated among his child soldiers, only maybe worse. Yellow eyes, jaundiced from repeated exposure to malaria, had a feverish glaze in them. Zygomatic bones jutted out defiantly against hollow cheeks. His lips were chapped, and his skin had an unnatural leathery look. He did not resemble a man for whom the gods of life had much use left. And if one got a glimpse of his surroundings, it became apparent that he was no General, and his was no militia but a ragtag assembly of lawless misfits. He looked mildly concerned at the brigand's state but was otherwise as nonchalant as the children.

"What is it, soldier?"

I killed a fellow comrade in the heat of argument, the brigand thought to say. His heart was pounding uncontrollably, and he was certain the boss was onto him. His knees began quivering under the weight of ten million tonnes of guilt. That familiar chill rose up his spine yet again. Before it could paralyse him, he blurted, "FARDC are coming. They have already reached Kwala village."

The boss shot up from his chair, now openly alarmed – and perhaps something less manful too. "What!? And you choose this moment to stammer!" He quickly put on a jacket, picked up a G3 leaning by the wall and dusted himself off.

Was that a hint of… fear?

"Get the troops ready. Tell the carriers to get all my things. We are moving!" This the boss told the child, who promptly disappeared. He shoved a MAS-49 upon the brigand as he walked out. "It's time for action, soldier. Get your squad! And for Christ's sake, where is Tukio!?"

The boss did not wait for an answer but was out the door before the brigand had a chance to mouth the word "dead." He seemed more invested in getting out of danger's way than in such trivialities as the whereabouts of his men, the General. Invisible scales fell from the brigand's eyes, but he was only just beginning to learn how to see. Slowly, penitently, his rugged breath became regular.

Trying to bite back the pain in his torso, he walked out into the open air. The commotion had followed like a bad spirit, getting closer to camp by the minute. His breathing became laboured. Pain shot up, radiating through the crown of his head and the heels of his feet; the adrenaline was washing away.

"All is fair in love and war," he murmured to no one.

He took a frail step and collapsed.

It was everywhere now; veins of blinding pain lit up his head, chest, arms and legs.

The avalanche had arrived.

Rapid shivers followed.

All is fair in… love and… war.

The world became bright.

Up in the empty sky, he saw a gloomy girl on the banks of a tropical river.

All is… fair… in… love… and… war.

The empty sky burned to a char of nothingness.

And as the brigand breathed his last, never having understood the meaning of the words, he repeated them.

All... i... fair...

Fatima Okhuosami

Fatima Okhuosami loves to transform her thoughts into short stories and poems. Her works are published with Isele Magazine, The Kalahari Review, Itanile Magazine, Jalada Africa, Writers Space Africa, and elsewhere. She was first runner-up of the 2020 Collins Elesiro Literary Prize and 2021 Kendeka Prize for African Literature, and longlisted for the 2022 Toyin Falola Prize.
She is on X (formerly Twitter) @fatiokhuosami. She also runs blogs at fatimetu.blogspot.com and fatimetu.mondoblog.org

God Created A Thing
Fatima Okhuosami - Nigeria

At the dawn of dusk on the sixth day, God created a thing. Feeble then strong. Buffoon then sage. Finite.

Under the shed beside our former central mosque, motorcycle riders and *agberos* gather every sundown to drink Mama Hope's ice-cold Guinness. Alongside beer, she sells ready-to-smoke cannabis loaded into cigarettes. We call her Mama Hope even though she is barren and the only child who lives with her is Itunu, brought from the village to help with chores, in exchange for feeding and housing. I remember asking my mother the story behind her friend's nickname. She told me something about a traveling pastor's prophecy, an immaculate conception, a rejected cervical cerclage, and the miscarriage that would have been Hope.

There's a tree stump carved like a stool in front of the wooden benches in Mama Hope's stall, near the main road. My brother and I used to perch on it, waiting for the seven o'clock bus to Benin. My brother who has been dead these ten years.

I keep my mother out of Annex C, Federal Neuropsychiatric Hospital, Benin, by reaching out morning and night without fail. Also, I adhere to a strict regimen of visiting every six months, *sallah* holidays included. But this Eid is different from its predecessors.

After *subh* prayers.

Before our landlord's goats bleat their good mornings.

When I should be peeling yams and boiling the chicken we'd eat while waiting for my uncle to slaughter our ram (his brother being the most yellow-bellied of men),

I do a peculiar thing.

Darkness is fading when I step out. Ma, dozing on a prayer mat, has wrapped her fingers tight around my sparkly blood-red *tasbih*. A sexagenarian with three wives and an uncertain number of children gifted it to me three months ago, upon his return from Saudi Arabia. I take a moment to study the many lines crisscrossing her face like double helixes. Ulcers at the junction of her lips. A second chin drooping like half a cellophane of water. They frighten me just like her white hair and weak knees and sudden intolerance for milk.

The sky is dawn's most constipated grey. Blasts of cold wind bounce against my calico *jilbab* as I move. It hisses its disapproval with every step. Mist coats the epidermis of my pink-rimmed prescription glasses for astigmatism. In what is now a drizzle, I find five children near a ditch, playing house. They all have wide jaws, knitted brows, and honey-brown skins signifying a familial relationship. I halt, ready to receive their greetings before sending them home, but the little rascals do not bother to acknowledge my existence. Respect and standards have gone to hell.

I was raised by these narrow red roads. Maroon houses wedded to rusted zinc roofs. *Obeche* and Tangerine trees doing life in harmony. Three equidistant rivers, each deeper than the next – a neighbour's kid drowned in one many years ago, but he was not quite right in the head so nobody, not even his parents, cared enough to search. The water spirit vomited him four days later. And we did not tell the adults that it was us who had dared him to jump.

Today, there are no friends to say with jealous smiles, "welcome back, how is city life?" Nor enemies to forgive for their slights. Whose are these faces I do not recognise?

I want to play *tinko-tinko* again. To laugh over the time I fell from Mr. Braimah's guava tree and broke both knees. I want it all back. Everything before Benin. That place which swallowed my brother, wrung his neck, and shat his corpse. It is a curse within me. This longing for things I can no longer have.

How we danced when Abdul finally gained admission to study medicine after three failed attempts. My mother recited one thousand *alhamdulillahs* and stayed up many nights praying away the evil eye. The *jumat* after we received his good news, she put five hundred naira in the offering bowl – a nine hundred percent increase on her usual subscription. Yet God did not tell us we were celebrating the beginning of his end.

The circumstances surrounding my brother's misfortune are as staggering as they are bizarre. I will walk you from facts to conjectures. Yes, he was *brought in dead* to the hospital by two hotel staff who "found him floating lifeless on our pool." They were forced into a confrontation at the hospital gates by a horde of inebriated young men in black and yellow robes. We made our way inside at about 10 p.m. and the nurses showed Abdul to us, his neck two times the normal size. A dried stream of blood was visible from the right junction of his lips to the edge of his jaw. The high cheekbones he inherited from my mother sank into his bloated face. Somebody had tied a string around his neck. On it, was a pendant bearing "BID" scrawled in blue ink.

We swore an affidavit not to carry out an autopsy before the mob allowed us to move his corpse. It rained the night we put him in the ground. Everybody said this was a good omen.

No, the friends he was with at the end (ranking members of the Buccaneers Association of Nigeria) did not follow his body to the hospital nor attend his funeral. In fact, I did not set eyes on any of them until three weeks after the event when one sought me out in my hostel because he needed to "transfer the movies I downloaded in Abdul's laptop."

Piecing together information from diverse sources, this is how I believe his last moments unfolded:

My brother, his friend, and a young lady are hanging out poolside. The men drink Heineken and their companion, Hollandia strawberry-flavoured yoghurt. There's chicken kebab on the table. My brother whispers into the girl's ear. She throws her head back and laughs, her entire frame jerking. He looks proud and somewhat surprised that this stunning creature finds his jokes hilarious. A party of nine guys stroll into the vicinity. The friend, facing the gate, lifts his arm to draw their attention. My brother turns, spots them, and seizes his date's hand. He tries to escape, but his friend blocks the way. The assailants approach. His friend joins them. The girl slips away. A quarrel ensues and eyewitnesses try to intervene but retreat when the men bare their weapons. The argument continues. They slap him, punch him, kick him. He staggers to his knees and begs for his life. A tear has decimated his lower lip. They push him into the water. He struggles. They wait until his arms cease flaying and the last bubble bursts. Then they turn around and leave.

I am recalled to the present by a boy nigh four feet tall, who, carrying a pressing iron filled with red hot coal, darts past me. He trips on a stone and tumbles to the ground, thankfully centimetres away from the instrument in his keeping. I help him up, dust his bleeding knees, and stare into his eyes. He has Abdul's mischievous scowl. An overwhelming urge to laugh consumes me. I embrace him and he shrinks a little, tries to free himself from my grip. When I release him, cackling with the full force of liberated madness, he flees.

Approaching a huge locust tree, I pause. Like the rain, my laughter ends abruptly. Clouds above me start to assume an exquisite turquoise. It was right here, on the way home from school, that I received my first real kiss… at thirteen. Followed by a hug so hard, my premature breasts shrank. This from my computer science teacher. Who was also our principal's brother. Why did he smile that coy smile and whisper, thick lips lightly grazing the hairs on my ear, "See, you like it," then add to my mortification by asking whether my prudishness was an act. *If I push a chicken egg inside your vagina right now, will it not fit?* I would have given all my pocket money for the ground to open up and swallow me. What imbecilic reasoning made me hide what he did from his friend, my father?

But how could I report when I henceforth, looked forward to his touch and covetously vied for his attention? He made me believe myself beautiful, a bona fide member of an elite syndicate of fair-skinned chicks from which he picked his girlfriends. This was an achievement far greater than ranking top three in class. Fatima did not have to write raging love letters or use S.V.C, the bleaching lotion that was the rave that year, in order to bag a man. And of all men, *him*.

I must have covered at least a quarter mile because I find myself at a crossroad. One footpath rears its head to the left, just before a kiosk manned by an easterner selling soft drinks. I watch him drop two crates of Coca-Cola, grab the back of his waist, then with visible effort, force himself into an upright position. This "uncle" who, one afternoon, many years ago, seized his girlfriend by the throat for daring to demand that he pay back the seventy thousand naira he borrowed from her. He locked the poor creature indoors and beat her within an inch of her life. Somehow, he managed to convince the entire neighbourhood to show up for his wedding… not long after… to another woman. She went on to give him two sons and her life.

There's a chewing stick in his mouth. "Good morning," I holla, without stopping. He nods his response, coughs, then spits a giant ball of phlegm. "Fati *mai mai*," he teases, using the moniker that has stuck to me since childhood. "Welcome back o. I go keep two crates for you." I will patronise him on my way back from the prayer ground.

Here and there, buildings sprout like beanstalks. They have solar panels on corrugated roofing sheets, a testament to new money. I detest them and their occupants with a venomous jealousy that makes the tips of my fingers itch. After seven years labouring for a "professional degree," followed by job stints across a myriad of private establishments, I am back with barely enough money to buy a new motorcycle for my father. Unlike my mates living it up in America, London, Ontario and Seoul.

My first visit post-employment, I bought three secondhand abayas for my mother and a rechargeable lantern for the house. The fellow who sold it to me promised it was the latest design – best in the market. All it needed, he swore, was sunlight for two hours per day. Even when it became obvious that this eleven-by-eleven cuboid monstrosity was more adept at serving as a haven for cockroaches than lighting up our house, my parents still pretended to be impressed.

At the end of the lane, Mr. Balogun's bungalow stands like a scarlet letter. I am confronted by a congregation of window-length weeds. The green paint has peeled off the walls, leaving behind a washed-out sickly yellow finish. I move towards the gate and push its broken bell. All at once, it is 2004 again and Rotimi Balogun just went into hiding. A foreseeable consequence of lopping off his sister's thumb with a cutlass. In his defence, Rotimi could not understand the audacity that made her serve him seedy pounded yam. Or why when questioned, against the rules of self-preservation, she insisted on speaking up for herself. Even threw a few insults his way. He aimed for her neck, but God as always, is merciful.

That Sunday night, the Baloguns brought Sonia to my father, our town's best nurse. Madam Ruth B. Opia was reporting the most attention-grabbing events of the week on *News Line*. Abdul and I willed the hands of the wall clock to speed up to ten o'clock when it'd be time for Papa Ajasco. The sudden appearance of a family bowed down by hysterics at our door, however, spiked our curiosity. This held more potential than Miss Kpekeye's bare bottom jeans and Boy Alinco's multilayered, poly-coloured spectacles.

When the commotion settled, I was conferred the honour of manning a torch while my father stitched flap to stump. I wonder if Sonia will recognise her saviour today. Eighteen years and a salad of illnesses have done terrible work on him.

Rotimi's exile threw his Aye confraternity into its worst leadership crisis, culminating in a month-long bloody war that claimed at least ten souls. Crucial steps were taken to run the rest of the family out of town. Today, over one decade after things fell apart, he is a supervisory councillor in the local government authority.

I cross to the other side of the expressway, stroll past our former apartment (now a poorly patronised guest house) and MTN's giant telecommunications mast. I don't stop until I am standing opposite the local government council gate. Here, I lock eyes with a tall, slim beauty selling *okpa* from a brown sack inside an aluminium basin riddled with rust. She has porcelain skin and wickedly luscious eyes. Something ravenous growls inside of me. There are six customers in line, two of which dawdle, I suspect, for an opportunity to ask her out.

This spot used to be Mama Antonia's bean cake stand. For twelve years, come rain or sunshine, the old woman made a living and fed her two grandsons, my brother's classmates, those grubs for breakfast. They'd grab three pieces each and rush off with us to school. Now my brother is dead. And Antonia too, of AIDS, a sickness that should not be fatal in big 2022.

The blended tones of Sister Sledge belting out lyrics from their 1985 hit, "Frankie," blast from my Samsung A71. I pull my gaze from the back side of Delilah, whisper a quick *zhikr* against temptation, and grab the impertinent device. It is my mother calling. Because her worrying is detrimental to our collective sanity, I hurry home the way I came, only to find her resting against a big rock in front of our burglary proof. She neither asks nor do I offer any explanation for my disappearance.

Silence, the uncomfortable kind, stretches between us as she measures forty-four cups of rice and I dice carrots. When I am done, I remove two cockerels from a bucket of hot water and start plucking feathers. I remember she used to silence me with the lie that talking causes more of them to appear, and grin.

There was a time when *sallah* mornings meant a kitchen filled with noises. Abdul would place himself on frying duty, then wrap his hands with rags to protect himself from oil spills. We'd joke, laugh, yell, force our mother to retell childhood stories, then tease her for their absurdity. My father would march into the kitchen to grab pieces of fried meat under the guise of ordering us to be quiet. Now my mother's stomach is a yawning abyss and its well of words has dried up. So, we sit in this lamentable stillness, each judging the other, me aware forcing conversation would hurt her. Would her life have been less difficult if I had gone instead of him?

With a sigh, I fortify the dam threatening to burst. Tears come to me easy these days. As if I fetch them from a depot, yet however much I take, it replaces itself tenfold.

I lower my head over steam from the bucket long enough to overcome successive waves of hypoglycaemia-induced dizziness. In the last twenty-five hours, nothing has passed my throat except one cup of black tea and half a slice of bread. When I sit up, I find my mother watching me, curiosity plastered over her face. *Ask me what is wrong*, I scream, wordlessly. *Talk to me. I am your daughter. You used to enjoy talking to me.* My head is filled with the bickering of one thousand angry Fatimas. It occurs to me that I might be a little bit mad.

As has been her habit for ten years, she refuses to attend Eid prayers. I wear a blue mermaid dress – one of AliExpress's black Friday offerings over red slingback heels. I wrap the keffiyeh she inherited from her mother in-law around my head and hand her my phone to snap pictures which I upload to twitter with trending hashtags. In less than five minutes, I receive seven retweets and five likes. But at the prayer ground, half an hour passes without anybody noticing me. In spite of the fact that I spread my mat super close to the main entrance, I am a speck of dust in a sandstorm. When the khutbah begins, I start to put names to some faces in the crowd.

Our late imam's eldest daughter bent double from the weight of her many years.

One of the teachers from my madrasa.

The second richest Muslim in our town flanked by his newest wife – presented to him straight out of secondary school, as a gift, by her father.

Then I see him. I cannot look away. He turns and his eyes clock mine. An army of goose pimples invade my skin. I itch in one thousand different places. Every breath seems forced out of my lungs. This man that I loved with the fervent adoration of pubescence for all of three years and maybe more. Time has been kind to him; he is chubbier, but not fat. Handsomer. The thickening of middle age becomes him well. Somewhere inside my brain, I record: soft oval face, taut muscles, skin the colour of burnt sugar. His tailored kaftan and leather shoes indicate a much higher rung in the prosperity ladder of our town. I envision the question on his lips, and I have prepared my answer. Each step in my direction saves, then damns me. Twenty. Fifteen. Five. Two. He is so close I can feel his breath caress my nose. My computer science teacher.

"Fati, is this you? The young shall grow o." His well-manicured fingers move towards my face, but they stop halfway, from what I imagine must be supernatural self-control.

"Salam alaykum sir." My eyes are downcast and tone, low-pitched. This is the way he likes his girls.

I learn he's been married twice in three years, both of which were childless and culminated in divorce. He shows zero emotion when I tell him I am *still in the market*. He's back in town he says, for a friend's wedding. The muezzin starts the call to prayer and we are caught in limbo. Somehow, I communicate with coquettish disinterestedness, that asking for my number will not be unwelcome. He takes the bait. My lips spread into a shy smile as I type the digits into his iPhone 14.

Although I am ready when his call comes in, fully dressed in pyjamas, under the duvet, earbuds plugged, my poor heart cannot help but thump. As soon as I hear that raspy voice say "baby," I drum my feet against the mattress in wanton joy. For most of the conversation, I barely speak, content to drink his words. Just after we wish each other sweet dreams, he confesses, "Maybe there is a reason my marriages failed. You are the woman God created for me." For a split second, my brain screams, "abort mission." But because I am evidently insane, in his confidence, I see stability … and rescue. From crippling loneliness, a string of terrible romances and hopeless talking stages. *This man loves me.* So, I do what a prey must never do. Nothing. And in that nothingness, I seal my fate.

Kudzai Parutu

Kudzai Parutu is a Zimbabwean writer and visual artist. She has a bachelor's degree in law from the University of Zimbabwe and her first book, 'Taembedzwa', was published in her second year of college. She was born and bred in Chipinge, and she grew to love everything about the Eastern Highlands – the culture, language, weather, mountains, people – everything. After graduating, she moved to Chimanimani, a place much colder than Chipinge with steeper hills, where she currently works as a Gender and Prevention from Sexual Exploitation and Abuse focal point for a community-based organization. Her social media handles are Parutu Ku – Facebook, Parutu Ku – Instagram.

The UY Club
Kudzai Parutu - Zimbabwe

The Unemployed Youth club. All it takes is following four prompts to exit the WhatsApp group, but it is pointless; in real life I remain an unyielding member of the UY club.

On some days I am impatient to cry, I snap at my mother and feel guilty about it seconds after. I cry under my blankets and ask God if this is what he planned for me. The truth is I am tired.

I do not know what my place is in this world. It's like everywhere I try to squeeze into, I'm swiftly spit out. But what frustrates me the most is I'm supposed to cultivate a space for myself on this dry land. Life has become a grocery list with items to be ticked off, and I stopped at "graduate". I have never put much thought into ticking off "get married", but "get a job" is definitely something I had hoped to.

And earlier.

At times, I ask myself, if my current state of affairs is this tough on me, what of my parents who gave their all to make sure I would be nothing but the best? Growing up, coming second was never an option. There were beatings, punishments like sleeping under the table or bathroom floors, slaps that left my cheeks throbbing; all these to panel beat me into the finest of my parents' productions. My father put our relationship on the stake, where it burned and died, to make sure I would either be a doctor or engineer. All that, so I could be an unemployed lawyer in their house. Perhaps I should be enjoying the bittersweet taste of my failure, for the satisfaction that comes from disappointing them.

There are five stages of being jobless. The first one is guileless hope, and I had an unhealthy dose of it in in the beginning – I am a law graduate after all. There is an uncle who asked for my resumé so he could see what he could do. Two years later, he is still seeing to it. There are rich men who preyed on college students, who dangled the countless connections they supposedly had in my face just so they could get between my legs.

And then, in the job applications, I flaunted all my talents, even the ones I do not have. When I sum it up, I wonder if companies ever really buy it. *I am a young woman who can work under pressure, overtime and whose weakness is prioritising her work over her social life.* I could as well claim to be Wonder Woman. This stage lasted only three months for me, squashed by a law firm I regret ever applying to.

The interview was my first ever, and I nailed it, which is to say I persuasively reinforced the blatant lies I had written in my resumé. They called to offer me the job a few hours later. The receptionist's voice crackled through my phone's microphone, and I had to piece together what she was saying as I paced around my rented room for a spot with good reception. I finally found a good spot just as she said, "You start on the first of February." I did my victory dance, my left hand hitting the sharp edge of the door in the process.

I had been unemployed for just three months, and in this moment, I was grateful for the five days of fasting my mother had partaken in on my behalf. I now had an incentive to spend the money that was standing between me and poverty, so I invested in formal shoes, formal clothes and handbags, and stowed aside just enough for transport to and from work for the first month.

The first of February couldn't come around fast enough. On the thirty-first of January, I ironed three of my favourite dresses, straightened my *sankita* wig and oiled it, packed my handbag, and debated whether it would be wise or not to wear heavy makeup on the first day. When morning came, I was in and out of the bathroom in under fifteen minutes. I chose a black dress, a black blazer, and wore my wig, the cap flattening my dreadlocks against my scalp. In front of the mirror, I took out my titanium tongue bar and replaced it with a pink, flattop plastic one that would be less conspicuous. I decided against makeup.

I was half an hour early, which gave me time to deal with my nerves before eight. Baba had sent me a link to a video about how to act on your first day of work, what to and what not to say. I decided not to watch it. My mother sent a message, wishing me the best on my first day of work, something I knew my father had put her up to. Not that she is the unfeeling type, she is just not the thoughtful type. She had obviously prayed for me when she woke up that morning, sending spiritual soldiers to people working against me, the group being highly populated by our relatives from my father's side, according to her. And in the bus to work, I knew, she had made it known to everyone that I was starting work at a prestigious law firm in the big city. She would have also taken note of everyone who didn't receive the news with enthusiasm and were supposed to join her list of haters.

I sent her back a string of hearts. Calculating the distance between the main gate and myself, I decided it was reasonable that I wore my heels there. They were not my favourite, but they were my most comfortable pair, and I was not going to risk having wobbly knees on the first day of work.

I took my time slipping into them and securing the belt around my ankle. A young boy with his ears plugged with codeless earphones pushed a cart encumbered with pineapples past me. The strong scent of pineapples wafted towards me, the fruit pleasantly redolent of home. I smiled wistfully, taking it as a good sign.

From the direction the boy had come from, there emerged a girl whose gait I recognised. She was walking briskly, her upper body thrust forward, which she did to draw attention to her round butt as my best friend had once said. Her name was eluding me, and I was still trying to remember it when she smiled, her lips parting to reveal her remarkably white teeth, and my mind stopped working. All I knew was that the name started with a T, and she was in the habit of pronouncing it like an English word instead of a Shona word. We were never friends, but we had been in the same groups in law school a few times that we had shared enough small talk to pretend we were. And every classmate becomes more special after school, in any case.

She looked like she was dressed for an interview, and she had gone for a modest look. She was trying to send a message, 'I am a good girl' in a pencil skirt that stopped quite a number of inches below her knees. Tucked into its waist was a long-sleeved blouse with a round collar that neatly closed around her neck. The clothes were loose, keeping their distance from her body. I wondered if she was hiding tattoos beneath them like I was. She could have looked less dishevelled if she had worn heels, but she had gone for flats, and the look had ended up communicating the opposite of what she intended. It was giving more of 'I don't care' than 'I won't sleep with the senior partner'.

Her wig seemed to have a mind of its own, facing upwards, prepared to bolt at the slightest brush of strong wind. She had pulled down her surgical mask, and it now cupped her chin, her face powder turning the sky-blue material brown. Convinced I looked better than her, I lowered my mask and smiled back at her.

"Tanyisa!" she exclaimed excitedly. The reaction threw me off, but I recovered in time to return the smothering hug and spread my cheeks into a huge reciprocal grin.

"How have you been?" I asked, not caring at all for the answer.

"Great, great. Wait, where are you working?" she looked around, absentmindedly tugging at her mask. She must have pulled hard, because the string hooked behind her left ear snapped and the mask came off on that side.

"There," I pointed towards the banner of the firm I was about to be indefinitely a part of in just a matter of minutes.

"Oh! Me too. When do you start?" She had now gathered the mask in her palm, and she gently unhooked it from the right ear.

Cheerfully, I said, "Today,".

"Me too," she said, her low voice betraying her waning excitement. It wasn't big enough a company to be hiring two interns at the same time. For some time, she focused on rummaging through her bag, then heaved a loud sigh when her hand came out with a clean, unused mask which she slowly wore.

"Oh, great. At least I will have a familiar face around," I tried to lighten the mood. Her eyes crinkled, which I interpreted to mean she had smiled at me. "Let's head up there, it's almost eight."

"No, they open at half past," she said confidently.

I was thrown off again. There was a nagging feeling at the back of my mind that maybe only one of us was wanted.

"Oh, how did you know…" I started asking but then stopped myself. It sounded more like a plea than a question.

"When I was waiting to be interviewed, one of the partners approached me and struck up a conversation. We have been in touch since. He is very friendly."

I could not believe what was happening in that moment. I looked around, searching for the pineapple cart, to remind me of home, but it was nowhere to be found. My feet were no longer appreciating standing still in heels, however comfy they were, so I insisted the two of us head up to the building.

There was an awkwardness that hung between us as we walked. I tried to comfort myself. It would be incredulous if I were to be fired; I had gotten the job, and they had given it to me!

The odds weren't in my favour, though. She had connections, I did not. I believed, then, that things would work out for me without moving any pieces. There were actually no pieces to move. Neither of my parents were connected in the legal field in any way. And, then, I was not willing to sleep with anyone for a job. Not knowing what was awaiting me, I led the way to the offices.

***

The second stage of joblessness is confusion. Simply not understanding what is happening, that is when you join groups like the UY club. But it passes quickly. What comes next is what no one sees coming. Paranoia. You start making an allowance for the possibilities of someone bewitching you. You start hoping your mother would drop the fervent prayers and take you to a witch doctor instead to identify the witch. After the first of February, everyone became a suspect in my eyes. I started conjecturing that my situation had been brought on by relatives jealous of my success as a degree holder. Stage four is despondency, which grips you so hard you can do just about anything for a job. Then there is resignation, which people deal with differently. I have become a philosopher. I upturn and question everything, then come up with theories that direct the blame elsewhere but my way.

My boyfriend is calling. He has a degree in Development Studies. He is on the same boat as I am, only he went through the stages pretty fast, and when he reached stage 5, he chose to find a 'hustle' instead. He is now a *hwindi*, a commuter omnibus conductor and has lately become very seasoned at hanging from speeding vehicles with one arm. His new work name is Bholato-Bholato. He wants me to have a 'backup plan', but I cannot think of anything. Selling clothes? Everyone is doing that now. Whenever I go on WhatsApp, it is like logging onto an online boutique.

I answer the call.

"Babe," I try to sound cheerful, but he knows better. He has been with me through the worst of days. He understands how I hate being the

43

centre of my mother's incessant prayers. He understands how I have tried but never gotten round to praying about my situation. He comprehends how I doubt this God, how I harangue myself with questions about a God who should never be questioned. He knows this makes me feel guilty to pray. So, he does the praying for me. He always listens as I recount my theories to him.

"I am taking an off day tomorrow. I have enough money for us to go for a picnic," he says. I can hear the traces of a smile in his voice. I realise I am smiling too.

"Okay, papi," I purr, earning a laugh from him. We both fall silent, and we stay like that, listening to each other's gentle breathing. The silence is soothing.

"I love you, Tanyisa," he says finally. I bite my lower lip, my eyes welling up.

If my life was to end today, I know how tomorrow would have unfolded. Every day, I wake up an hour after my mother has left for work. That is after fighting to sleep through the pandemonium of her preparing for work. She switches my light on and off a thousand times so she can check her outfits in my mirror, the door creaking loudly every time she comes in. And then a few minutes before she leaves, she stands in my room, reciting all the chores I have to do throughout the day even though I know them by head. The first few minutes of being awake, I drag my feet around the house, dusting, sweeping, mopping. I only become fully awake when I go outside to do the dishes from the previous night. Then, I am left with nothing to focus on except unemployment depression.

I avoid Facebook these days, it has been overrun by my classmates getting registered as legal practitioners. I am easily triggered by the reiterative posts of a smiling human in an overflowing graduation gown, a milky white jabot strangling their thirst away, and standing in front of the scales of justice at some High Court in the country. The picture always has the same redundant caption beginning with, "Let it be known to all men whom it may concern…"

."I love you Bholato-Bholato," I whisper and get a throaty laugh. My mother approves of him simply because he has a degree and hasn't resorted to stealing – he is a real man. I always tell him this and it exhilarates him that even though that's not his definition of a real man, at least someone thinks he is.

***

The workers started trickling in around nine. I kept an eye out for the friendly partner, but I couldn't identify him. T, next to me, was furiously typing on her phone. I figured it had everything to do with the little situation we had found ourselves in. And I could tell she was double texting with no shame whatsoever. At some point, it seemed like she was the one who was sending texts without getting any responses.

The receptionist arrived; a mid-thirties woman overtly generous with her smiles. She remembered T, from the interview she said. She called her by her name, Tanya; only the owner made a point to pause after the 'n' and pronounced it as "Ten-yeah".

Tanya started feeding me information about whoever passed, her source being the friendly partner. The girl in black slacks had just made partner, had a car and lived in the suburbs; the other girl was an associate, having affair with the senior partner– she had no car. That boy? Oh, that was one of the partners' son, only there for the Wi-Fi.

She went back to her phone after that, leaving me to find comfort in studying the designs on the carpet. And then I realised it had suddenly become eerily quiet. The receptionist was nowhere to be found and Tanya was perched up on the couch, her body taut. She seemed to be holding her breath, waiting for something to happen. I wondered what was expected of me in that moment, if was I supposed to be tense too. But all I felt was just impatience.

The senior partner finally appeared; I remembered him from the interview. He stood by the door that led to the offices, his large frame crowding it. He wore a grey suit, white shirt and blue tie. His blazer was held together by a dented button that was loose and on the verge of popping off. I could make out the loose thread. He had outgrown his beard. In that moment, it was evident he was annoyed.

"Hello, girls, follow me." He turned on his heels and headed towards his office. I led the way, Tanya trailing behind. I felt a surge of anger towards her for something I couldn't put a finger on. In the office, the man stood behind his desk, packing documents in those suitcases lawyers drag to court to look more qualified than they are. "Girls, sit down," he ordered.

We did.

Somehow, I ended up in the same seat I sat in during the interview. He remained standing, peering down on us. I realised something about him got on my nerves.

"There has been…" he searched for a word, but I knew what was coming anyway "…an adjustment. In the beginning, we intended to hire both of you, but now things have changed. So only one of you stays. Go decide outside," he spread the tips of his fingers on the table. A laugh bubbled inside me. Could he hear himself? He really thought there was someone between the two of us or among all the unemployed youth of this country who would want to go back to being a home defender?

Still, we made our way outside, shoulders sagged and eyes downcast.

"So, what do we do?" I asked her once we were outside, standing next to the 'reception' sign. I was not sure it was the most proper thing to say given the situation.

"Ha! You think I am going to say I go home? And you stay! I…" she stopped, swiped across her phone and brought it to her ear.

Well, that was unexpected. I couldn't figure out why it was me she was angry at. Clearly, she had a plan with the friendly partner, and I must have caused a wrinkle in it by showing up. I recalled the call from the receptionist in my mind, questioning if I had heard correctly. I was sure I had…

"They said we should decide who stays and who goes home, otherwise he fires us both," she was telling the person on the phone.

He had not said the last part. I decided not to say another word to her again, since she had switched to the foul version of herself. Bholato-Bholato would later explain to me that Tanya must have been at stage four of joblessness.

I took out my phone, thinking of ranting to my best friend, but I didn't even know how to start. So, I shoved it back into my bag and leaned against the wall. After a while, the sound of heels walking on the pavement invaded my thoughts and I looked up to see the receptionist approaching. Tanya dropped her call and stepped closer to me.

"Have you decided, guys?' the receptionist asked, the smile still on. I wondered if, to her, a smile was an expression of emotion, or just a job description she was intent on upholding. We both shook our heads – I feared for Tanya's wig. "Come in, let me help you," she offered. Awash with relief and hope, I followed them back into the office. "I will write a 'yes' and 'no' card and you pick," she announced as we stood by her workstation.

For the second time that day, I felt a strong urge to laugh. So, it was now down to luck... Or was it? Still, I stood there, waiting for her and then she brought the cards to us. We both picked at the same time, but Tanya held hers daintily in her hand, bringing her other hand above the paper as if praying over it. I waited for what felt like a whole minute, but she made no move to open hers. This was being drawn out longer than I could bear, so I opened mine, which was written a big, bold NO.

"Well, your time will come," the receptionist said, her voice echoing in my head. I almost jumped. I had not noticed she had been hovering behind me the entire time like a spell of bad luck. Tanya dropped hers since she had obviously picked the 'yes'. I picked up her paper; why litter? And then I left the place in a haze. How? How? How to tell my family and friends? Like it is?

Like it is.

I composed a message I would paste in everyone's inbox later except my father's because he needed to be talked to in more formal English. He is just like that. I got to the task of sending these messages as I walked to the nearest shopping centre. I got responses that intensified the lump that had lodged itself in my throat:

It is not God's time yet.

Your job will come.

You deserve better, don't you worry.

And bible verses, and motivational quotes. My mother told me not to take it to heart, and she would tell me what she once did when she lost her job, which she followed up with a long voice note. She had gotten pregnant, and in those days, that was basis for termination of employment. After signing the papers, she lay down on the floor in the boss's office and cried her heart out. She wrapped up the voice note by reminding me not to cry, my job was being prepared by God. My father said it wasn't meant to be. I understood I would never know what he really thought; our relationship has always been like that, formal and boring.

At the Westgate shopping centre, I found a bench and ignored how hot the metal was as I sat on it. I took out the bread I had packed for lunch and devoured it. When my stomach was full and ready for the task at hand, I took out my lime-green face towel, buried my face in it and started crying. My body shook as I cried, coming undone. I had not known it then, but that is when the paranoia kicked in. What I had just experienced felt like an attack. After what felt like forever, I finally stopped, tired and drained. I stood up to look for transport home. That is when the two papers fluttered to the ground, still folded neatly. I picked them up to throw them in the bin. Something told me to open Tanya's. I did so.

It was also written, NO.

Sibongumusa Ncube

Sibongumusa is a twenty-four-year-old Zimbabwean aspiring writer whose experience includes three consecutive wins in the Cover to Cover Short Story Writing Competition (2012-2014), Intwasa Writing Competition finalist (2020), a selected participant for the Writing Women's Leadership in Southern Africa: Writeshop and Writer's Residency (2022) and a poem published in the Alaska Quarterly Review (2022) during her time in Alaska, USA as an exchange student. She is an International Relations major whose human rights and social justice activism extends to her writing.

Instagram: @seed_of_athena
X (formerly Twitter): @SeedOfAthena
LinkedIn: Sibongumusa Ncube

Lafa Elihle Kakhulu[1]

Sibongumusa Ncube – Zimbabwe

There is an untold story in a village in southern Zimbabwe that will catapult Vee from an inexperienced intern to a staff writer at the Atlanta Times. When she pitched it to her superiors, they booked her on the first flight back home and made it clear that they were taking a considerable risk on her, one they did not want to regret. She knew what that meant: come back with a compelling story or don't come back at all. But today is her last day in the village and no one has been willing to tell the story she came searching for. Two weeks after arriving, Vee is seen heading towards the local bus stop, silky loose blouse blowing in the hot, unforgiving air. She has to pull down her pencil skirt every few steps each time it rides up her legs, and she chides herself for packing it in the first place. Jeans would have been an equally inappropriate clothing choice but at least her legs wouldn't be coated with a film of stubborn dust. She wears a headwrap to feign modesty, but the luscious locks of the Brazilian weave on her head spill out of it and cascade down her shoulders. The arched eyebrows on her face have been drawn on, and several layers of foundation and toner have contoured her nose to half its size. Her face is screwed up in concentration as she pretends not to notice all the stares and glares thrown in her direction as she makes her way through the worn-out paths in the grass. She almost fails to notice the little boy who excitedly runs up to her and exclaims that his grandfather wants to see her. He has a story to tell.

She follows him and his incessant chatter into a homestead that looks no different from the rest except for a giant *msasa* tree in the centre under which sits an old man on a wooden stool, his walking stick leaning against the tree's trunk. She nervously approaches him and kneels on the reed mat next to him, stretching out her hand in greeting before the timid "*Salibonani*" she exhales punctuates the silence around them. He doesn't take it. Instead, he asks her what her name is, and she almost says Vee before she remembers she's in Zimbabwe, so she can use her full name without having to smile awkwardly and say "No, you didn't butcher it, that's actually close!". Vuyisile. It tastes strange in her mouth,

---

[1] *a Ndebele translation of, "Cry, the beloved country" or more directly translated as "The death of a beautiful nation*

like a favourite childhood dessert that soured with age. He stares at her, prompting her to continue, because her introduction is incomplete. She is Vuyisile Dube from Magedleni village in Matshetsheni, the people that call themselves "*abathwali bophahla*[1]". This sounds more impressive in her head because the words tumble out awkwardly on account of the American accent she has acquired over the years.

He nods his head like she's confirmed a long-standing suspicion and says his name is Ndlovu, marking the beginning and end of his introduction. Vuyisile cannot help but smile. Her mother's maiden name is Ndlovu. She knows his clan names and stares him down while she rattles them off. *Gatsheni. Mthombeni. Boyabenyathi.* She expects him to look impressed, or at least taken aback, but his face continues to reveal nothing. After a prolonged beat of silence, he stretches out his hand to shake hers. She gives him her rehearsed introduction about how she's a writer working with the Atlanta Times, and she's been sent here on assignment to write about the Gukurahundi genocide and how the community is recovering forty years later. He reads in between the lines and hears everything else she doesn't say. She is here to capitalise on this community's grief by masquerading as one of them. But she has no roots in this community, she does not identify with them or their pain, at least not past a point where she can use it to climb up the professional ladder. She's a vulture here to feed on the scabs of his injuries and they both sit in the acute awareness of this fact.

There's a long, drawn-out silence while he ponders what to do. She's about to leave, uncomfortable with the awkwardness of it all when the old man flinches. A stone's throw away, behind the hut that bears all the tell-tale characteristics of a kitchen, his teenage granddaughters are pounding millet. They raise the pestles as high as they can go and forcefully bring them down until the grains disappear, and only a powder remains for cooking *isitshwala samabele* for lunch. Each time the pestle makes contact with the wide wooden bowl the millet is in, a dark shadow crosses his face. The untold story is beginning to find its voice. All of a sudden, it becomes too real for her. She has heard the reports of

____

[1] *the collective totem of villagers from Matshetsheni, meaning "the ones assigned to carry the roof", referring to the battalion of soldiers stationed there who were the first line of defence against enemies from the south for the Ndebele kingdom during the reign of Mzilikazi and Lobengula*

how the soldiers used to beat the villagers with pestles, their log-like size a perfect tool to break backs. "They're spineless cowards anyway, so we're not doing much damage", the soldiers would joke. Vuyisile wants to leave. This is not a story. These are real people with real pain, and she refuses to be the gravedigger who excavates all that buried suffering. She has crossed many an ethical line in her short career, but she cannot fathom coming back from it. She's about to get up when the man clears his throat and starts to speak.

He hesitates, unsure of where to begin. He doesn't look at her but steadies his eyes on the distant mountains. The first thing he says is that the girls are not his biological granddaughters. It pains him to say this because he loves them dearly and sees them as his flesh and blood, but his story is incomplete without stating this fact. He had three children of his own, two boys and a little girl he only got to hold for a week. When the soldiers grabbed him and took him to the concentration camp, his first wife went into hiding with the children. "She must have done a really good job of it too, because forty years later, they're still hiding," he says with a mischievous smile. Vuyisile is unsure of what the appropriate response is, but he's not looking at her so she doesn't react. She knows they're probably dead and wonders how often that realisation must have dawned on Ndlovu. To say they died would mean he would have to think about how they died. It's common knowledge that even little boys were rounded up, made to dig their graves, and once inside, were shot in the head. And that's if they were lucky. Most times, they were burned alive in the shallow graves. In both instances, their families would be held at gunpoint and told to sing and dance around the graves. Anyone who objected was shoved into the grave too. He could survive the thought of his wife singing at his sons' graves but what would break him is what happened to the baby. There were whispered rumours of babies being thrown against walls and newborns placed into wooden bowls with their mothers instructed to pound them to a pulp.

The girls interrupt them. They bring a jug of water and a bowl to wash their grandfather's hands.

As is custom, they kneel before him. Usually, a visitor would be the first to have their hands washed but Vuyisile is a woman and she's younger than him, so he ranks above her in this unwritten social hierarchy. He shakes his hands dry, and the girls kneel in front of Vuyisile who hesitates. It would be rude to refuse to eat their food, but she can also tell they don't have much of it to spare. She makes a split-second decision to accept the food and lets them pour the warm water over her hands and she feels a tinge of guilt when she realises it's borehole water. The nearest borehole being several kilometres away, the girls would have had to get up at the crack of dawn. Around here, every home carefully rations their water, and the case would be no different in this home. The two girls exchange giggles as they walk away, and the only word she catches from their hushed conversation is *umAmerican*. She looks like one, walks like one, and talks like one. And as she sits here, capitalising on the grief of a disenfranchised community for her gain, she feels more like one than on the day she passed her citizenship test.

He explains that he met the girls' grandmother in the Bhalagwe concentration camp. Like him, she had fought in the liberation war against the colonial Rhodesian government. They had sacrificed everything, dropping out of school and crossing the country's borders to go train in military camps in neighbouring countries. They had spilled so much blood, seen so much death, and done terrible acts all so they could reclaim the land that was rightfully theirs. And against all odds, they had won. Rhodesia was given back to the people and rechristened as Zimbabwe, the fabled house of stone. But the story never ends there, does it? It didn't in France, it didn't in Russia, and it didn't in Zimbabwe. With no enemy to fight, the war turned inward, and a revolutionary turned despot tried to create a one-party state and sought to erase the tribes that stood in his way.

They called it Operation Gukurahundi, the name given to the early rains that wash away the chaff before the spring rain. Like a violent storm, the state's army rolled into villages and left a trail of destruction in their wake. The Fifth Brigade were not ordinary soldiers. They were a specialised task force that received special military training in North Korea. Yes, *that* North Korea. They said they were looking for dissidents, soldiers who had not laid down their arms and were causing trouble in the villages. Ndlovu and every other Ndebele-speaking guerrilla who had fought in the war were dragged from their homes under the cover of the night. He cannot forget the night they came to his village, even though he has spent the last forty years trying. His first memory is of the smell of smoke mingled with the stench of burning human flesh. The state soldiers had found out that the neighbours were harbouring two guerrillas, so they locked the whole family into one hut and set it alight.

Ndlovu shook his wife awake and told her to run. Needing no other explanation, she leapt out of bed, grabbed the boys by their arms, and told them to quickly put on their shoes. They were dazed and confused, irritated at being woken up in such a violent manner, and stared at her blankly. She slapped them both across the face, screaming in their faces that this was not a game. Terrified, they did as they were instructed. She picked up the four-year-old and carried him on her back and put the baby in the eight-year-old's arms. The last Ndlovu ever saw of them was their shadows disappearing into the forest at the edge of their home. He took off in the opposite direction, thorny branches scratching his arms and rocks digging into his bare feet as he plunged deeper and deeper into the forest. He had just come from one war, and had not made it out alive of that one just to die in his own home. If they captured him, he wanted it to be in the next village. But he never even made it to the other side of the forest.

The girls arrive with the food and the conversation comes to an abrupt stop. Vuyisile's heart stops racing when she realises that she is safe and there is no one coming to get her. She had gotten so absorbed in the story, she has to double-check to see if her phone is still recording. The plates are placed before them and the two of them eat in silence. She scoops up some of the *isitshwala* with her fingers, dips it in the soup, and blows on it tenderly before eating. The whole act makes her self-conscious. A real native would eat the food piping hot without even flinching, or so she's observed. She hasn't had *isitshwala* since her family left the country when she was eight, and she can't remember if it always tasted like spoiled oatmeal. She attempts to gnaw on the chicken feet but there's barely any meat on it. Heart in her stomach, she eats every morsel and drains a cup of water to keep the nausea at bay.

The girls come to clear the plates and their grandfather asks for one of them to grab his straw hat. He suggests they go on a walk and Vuyisile is all too happy to agree. The pattern of the reed mat has imprinted onto her skin, and it hurts at the touch. Her legs also feel sore from the awkward position she has been sitting in. She rises to her feet, and they slowly walk out the gate together in what is now a comfortable silence. He's probably only in his early sixties, but his face is creased with wrinkles. He walks at an awkward angle and would undoubtedly crumple to the ground without his walking stick. He still grimaces with every step, and she feels an odd sense of protectiveness kicking in. Before she has time to dwell on this feeling, he points to a clearing in the distance. It's the local primary school. "School" is an exaggeration. There's just a tree with a blackboard underneath. The state of education in the whole region is abysmal.

"You know why?" he asks. She shakes her head.

"Then you're not as smart as I thought because I just told you," he says with a mischievous smile on his face.

She's seen a lot of truly atrocious things in her line of work, but this story feels personal. Maybe because it *is* personal. She cannot understand how a government could slaughter over twenty thousand people and get away with it and she says so aloud.

"Twenty thousand?" he scoffs. "That's what they told you?"

She is not entirely sure who "they" are, but she knows he is right. That was just the official number, but there was no way to verify those figures. Even now, so many families are still too scared to come forward because they believe their silence is the only thing keeping them alive. The day they talk is the day the soldiers come back, and no one is willing to risk that. Except for Ndlovu, a ghost of a man with nothing to lose.

He says there were at least eight hundred people in the month that he was at the concentration camp. There were soldiers posted everywhere so the prisoners could not even contemplate the very notion of escaping. They were divided into men and women to accommodate the unique systems of torture used to brutalise their bodies. Ndlovu discloses how all the men were subjected to castration during their stay.

"There's already enough of you people," the soldiers would smirk before bringing a hammer down on a prisoner's groin.

Or they would get creative and use electrocution. He spots the sympathetic look on Vuyisile's face and promptly changes the topic. He explains that the women had it worse. They were raped daily and brutally beaten up afterward, the soldiers taking out their disgust at themselves on the women whose evil powers of seduction were obviously to blame and were clearly genetic if the popular "*MaNdevere mahure*"[1] slurs on online platforms, newspaper cartoons and college campuses are

---

[1] *a derogatory slur identifying Ndebele women as promiscuous*

to be believed. Some of the prisoners were released when they got pregnant. The others were killed. It is hard to say which group was luckier. His second wife was part of the former. This is how Vuyisile concludes that the grandchildren Ndlovu is raising in his home are the descendants of his torturers.

The pair arrive at the bank of a muddy river, and Ndlovu leans against a rock so he can catch his breath. Vuyisile is unsure whether it's from narrating his trauma or from their long, leisurely walk. She slips off her sandals and wades into the water until it reaches the hem of her skirt. He calls her, but she keeps going deeper. She got in because she wanted to get rid of the red dust on her legs, but she can't explain why she keeps on going. She just knows this is where she belongs. In the Shangani river, where the last king of the Ndebele disappeared into mist. Where the bones of forgotten warriors are mingled with the remains of nameless corpses whose deaths were never officially recognised. Maybe she wants to find them and rescue them. Or more likely she wants to apologise for leaving home and never coming back. She is in a trance that is only broken when Ndlovu calls her Vuyi. There is some familiarity in how he calls her by a nickname she hasn't heard in years. She turns around and waddles out of the river. She tells him that her flight back home leaves tomorrow. He says nothing and starts to walk back to the village. She calls out and asks him if he knows if there is an opening for a new teacher at the school under the tree. He smiles and says there is. She smiles back and starts to follow him home.

Elias Muonde

Elias Muonde is a writer and journalist based in Harare. He also writes scripts for film, television and radio. For him, writing is a safe space for expression, escape and experiment. His work is biased towards the unheard voices of society, social and political justice.

Dolls
Elias Muonde – Zimbabwe

Chipiwa saw the last of her dolls on the morning following the nightmare.

Old pulling stockings stuffed with rags, hand sewn and tied into a feminine figurine, the doll was complete with real strands of braids salvaged from the stinking, rubbish dumb behind the new wood and tin saloon at Tsiga Store. It had a pair of sparkling eyes made from unusually large buttons ripped off an old jersey she had found in her grandmother's pillow. It was those eyes that made her love the doll more than the other dolls, never mind that everyone, including her grandmother, laughed at the doll, saying the eyes were hideous and wrongly sewn onto the forehead. She thought they were just jealous and hateful, because when she looked at the doll, its eyes were not on the forehead but right where they should be. At night, the doll's eyes would glow in the darkness just like those of Dada the stray cat roaming the alleys of Majubheki Line every night.

She had named the doll Tate, and everyone would ask her if it was short for Tatenda and she would vehemently shake her head, "no," Tate was just Tate.

Apart from Tate, Chipiwa had had several other dolls, each made from a different material, each made in a different style, each having its own personality and identity.

One was made from a piece of hessian sack cleverly folded into both figure and dress, crude to both eye and touch. It had long legs of mulberry twigs projecting from underneath the coarse dress. All this doll could ever do was stand when the twig legs were stuck into the sand or lie down on its back or side.

Another doll was made of maize cobs tied together by tiny wires then padded all over with a cotton cloth. This doll could only sit.

And there was one made of rags but covered on top with a white lacy fabric she had salvaged from the cuttings of the tailor woman operating from the veranda of Tsiga Store, Mai Gezimati. The doll was longish and delicate to both eye and touch. When Chipiwa had finished making this doll, she had realised the head was too small, so she had tried to help the situation by attaching large earrings to either side of the head. But the earrings, a rusty bolt and a nut she had unearthed from the dirt near the gate to their small house while sweeping the yard, were too heavy for the petite head and caused it to slump to the side. Instead of being disconsolate, she found it rather amusing and thought of the doll as a shy girl, one always with her head bent to the side.

Then there was Bhebhi, the plastic doll. Unlike the other dolls, Bhebhi was a "real" doll with pink skin and yellow hair and long legs and a smooth body and blue eyes and large eyelashes and a long arm. That was the problem with Bhebhi. She only had one arm and a hole where the missing arm should have been. At first, it didn't bother Chipiwa that the doll had one arm. She had found Bhebhi dumbed in the street on a rainy afternoon as she walked home from school, alongside an inflatable ball. She had picked the doll and left the ball, which she thought was too big to fit into her tiny red satchel, already full, with her shoes and a Maths textbook. Besides, who needed a ball when all they just wanted was to play by themselves?

Her grandmother had named the doll Bhebhi, because, she said, the doll had nice pale skin and smooth hair and beautiful large eyes and a stylish pose just like a real street *bhebhi*, attracting all the attention and whistles from hoodlums standing at street corners. Chipiwa had no problem having a doll who hogged the limelight from Mbare's hoodlums.

The problem only started when, a week after starting her Grade Seven, a new girl was added to their class. Her name was Barbra, and she had light skin and silky hair and long, slender arms and legs. She was talkative and everybody liked to be with her. Soon, she was made class monitor and her popularity and influence spread fast like a flu, but Chipiwa didn't catch the cold. She resented Barbra for some reason she didn't know. Maybe because her name sounded like Bhebhi. Maybe because she looked like Bhebhi. Then Chipiwa started being bothered by Bhebhi having one arm. She hated the hole on the side of the shoulder where the other arm should have been. She couldn't bear looking at it.

One night, when there was no electricity and grandmother had made a fire in the brazier to cook the evening's sadza, she shoved Bhebhi into the brazier headfirst and listened, with sardonic savour, to the searing and popping sound of plastic melting away under the blaze. Then, at an impulsive afterthought, Chipiwa pulled out the doll from the fire, dunked it into the tin of boiling water on the brazier and doused the flames. She held the doll before her eyes and suddenly burst into laughter. Without the head, Bhebhi looked funny and stupid, like those naked, life-sized dolls she had seen at Copacabana Flea Market in town. After laughing her heart out, Chipiwa flung the doll on top of the asbestos roof of the house. That was the last she saw of Bhebhi. The next school week was also the last she saw of Barbra. The popular girl suddenly stopped coming to school just before the class registered for the final exams. Rumours were that she had been discovered to be pregnant by the Head Teacher who took her to Edith Clinic for inspection. Rumour also had it that her father was responsible for the pregnancy, but another rumour said the man was her mother's boyfriend.

These dolls were all Chipiwa had for friends. Not that there were no girls of her age in Majubheki Line to be friends with; there were plenty of them in the streets surrounding her home and at school, but she found the dolls preferable to actual girls who could walk and talk. Her dolls were loyal, quiet, and funny. She always found them right there on the place she left them. And when they "misbehaved" during play time, she would discipline them by scolding or pinching them and they would not retaliate, sulk or wander away to other streets to look for other friends to play with and badmouth her.

But one late afternoon, Chipiwa came home from writing her last Grade Seven paper to find her dolls had wandered away.

She had left them piled behind her grandmother's house, in the tiny space between the wall and the low hedge marking the boundary with the neighbouring house. This tight cranny served both as a storage and dumbing corner for the people who lived at the house. It was where her grandmother kept her pile of firewood and planks salvaged from the carpenters near Mbare Musika Market. It was where her grandmother laid her petticoats and scrunched knickers to dry when she washed them after late afternoon baths. It was where all the now useless household stuff was dumped: the rusting metal thing with legs like a table which her grandmother said was once a coal stove, a steel frame of what was once a pram, rusty paraffin stoves covered in cobwebs, a piece of old carpet shoved into the clutter like a stub of tobacco, a bulgy hessian sack with unknown things that threatened to pierce their way out of the sack and tell the truth about what they really were and a brown suitcase with its steel fasteners clipped on, with large holes from years of being gnawed on by rats on all four corners. There was also a haul of Chibuku Super and Zambezi Lager bottles recklessly discarded about the entire place.

She had always left her dolls in this safe nook for as long as she could remember and would always return home to find them patiently waiting for her in the same spot, maintaining the same posture, not an inch amiss.

But today, they were gone.

She searched everywhere imaginable and unimaginable, every corner possible and impossible, but still there wasn't any sign of her dolls.

It was not until sunset that she learned about the sad fate that had befallen her dolls. Her grandmother had charged into the tiny yard, her hunched guise buckling under the weight of a heavy, stained sack which Chipiwa knew from the smell coming from it was *fodya*. Her grandmother wasn't that old, but she was already hunched and often joked that she was going to need a walking stick before the end of the year. The woman from next door, Mai Gezimati, the tailor, always said grandmother's back was prematurely bent by the heavy burden of life which she shouldered by herself. When she said the words "heavy burden", Mai Gezimati would train her eyes on Chipiwa. But grandmother would dismiss the joke by reminding Mai Gezimati that she had her first child when she was just thirteen and had gone on to bear seven more. There was no way in the world a woman's back would remain straight as a ladder after all that childbearing.

Upon sighting Chipiwa, who was still in her school dress, seated on the tiny stoep of the house with her head drooping to the side like Shy Bride the doll, grandmother exploded like a boil under a sweltering October sun. Words oozed out of her mouth like cess. Nasty words. Angry words. She asked her why she had not taken off the uniform, and Chipiwa said she no longer had use for the uniform since she had just finished writing her Grade Seven exam that afternoon. Her grandmother dropped the sack of *fodya* onto the veranda floor and asked Chipiwa if she had taken out the pots and plates from last night for washing, When Chipiwa told her she hadn't done that, grandmother asked what then had she spent the whole bloody afternoon doing, and when Chipiwa told her she had been desperately searching for her dolls, she became incensed.

"Your stupid little dolls are up there!" her grandmother had said, pointing a twitching finger at the roof.

Chipiwa looked up but all she could see was the aged grey of the asbestos sheets that made the roof of the house. She imagined her dolls strewn randomly across the flat roof, among the bits and clutter of old bicycle frames, car tires and shrunken shoes that were dumped there and forgotten about for lifetimes.

"No more dolls, you are no longer a baby!" her grandmother had declared, seizing the sack furiously in both hands and emptying the *fodya* onto the floor.

A pungent, musty smell filled the air as grandmother spread the deep brown, contorted tobacco leaves across the red floor of the veranda with her foot. Once or twice a week, she and a handful of other grandmothers from Majubheki Line would go to the Chinese owned tobacco factory across Simon Mazorodze Rd to glean condemned sheaves of tobacco, which were dumbed in a huge skip bin outside the high walls of the factory. The grandmothers from Majubheki Line would rescue the *fodya* from the skip bin, quickly fill their sacks and rush back home to spread the *fodya* in the sun so that it would be crispy and smokable. They would sell the *fodya* in measures of 5 litre pails for a dollar to the boys, men and grandfathers of Majubheki Line who couldn't afford the luxury of boxed cigarettes from street-side vendors and tuckshops.

That night, Chipiwa ate very little and went to bed early. She felt a heaviness inside her chest and a lump in her windpipe. She missed her dolls and struggled to fathom how she was going to live without them. She was wide awake until midnight when, suddenly, a downpour broke out of the sky and started pounding the earth. The first rain of November. She covered her ears with her arms so that she couldn't hear the noise the rain was making on the roof. The thought of the rain falling in swathes on the roof and drenching her dolls made her cringe.

The next day, Chipiwa's grandmother had woken her up very early in the morning and ordered her to grab a hoe under the pile of firewood in the junk corner at the back of the house and "follow me to the field near the railway line." The rains had come early, and only the early bird catches the worm, her grandmother had said. They had to start clearing the maize patch and dig planting holes before someone came to claim the patch as theirs, as is the norm here in Harare.

Still feeling the heaviness inside her inner cavities, Chipiwa got up and tottered out to the backyard in the darkness of the dawn. The tower light from near the bus rank, which usually bathes its immediate and distant vicinities in dazzling yellow, was not lit this morning, in fact, hadn't been lit for the past few days, so the whole backyard was pitch-black.

Chipiwa didn't remember using the hoe recently. She wasn't even sure there was any hoe in this corner, so she nonchalantly stretched out her hand into the wood pile hoping to get hold of the hoe by any chance.

As she was blindly groping for the handle of a hoe, Chipiwa found two pairs of glowing eyes staring at her from the dark bottom of the wood pile. She almost screamed but held back the scream when she realised it was only Dada, the stray cat from next door. Having had its night sanctuary inadvertently invaded, the big black cat meowed complainingly and scampered out. Dada was gone, but still there was another pair of eyes glowing at her, right close to where Dada had been laying. Chipiwa maintained her gaze on the glowing eyes, and soon, her vision became more acquainted with the darkness. The eyes were rather stationary and looked familiar.

The lump inside her throat immediately melted when Chipiwa realised what the source of the glowing eyes was!

She quickly reached her hand forward and retrieved Tate, her beloved doll.

How Tate had found herself under the wood pile in the company of Dada, Chipiwa didn't care to know. She was just happy at least one doll had survived the unprecedented banishment to the roof top.

For the few months that followed, Chipiwa enjoyed Tate's company in secrecy. She would tie her to her back and shield her from her grandmother by wearing a jersey or a jacket over her. She would go through all the digging and ploughing at the maize patch near the railway line, do all household chores, and go to Tsiga Store to buy Lacto or candles with Tate.

At day end, when she took her bath in the small lavatory, she would take the time to fix a loose strand of braid on Tate, re-tie her waist area to make her feminine figure more defined or hold her pressed to her cheek.

At night, she laid Tate beside her on the old sofa in the sitting room that had been her bed since she was old enough to sleep separate from her grandmother, and made herself careful not to roll over her during sleep.

But one night she wasn't so careful. She had a nightmare which caused her to roll back and forth on the sofa, squashing Tate, before falling off the sofa to the floor. In the nightmare, Chipiwa dreamt of three big, dark silhouettes of men chasing her down the railway track near her grandmother's maize patch. The track, with its bed of loose stones between the steel tracks, made running very difficult, and in no time, the silhouettes had caught up with her and pinned her down to the rough tracks. Chipiwa wrestled for freedom, but the silhouettes where just too powerful for her. She tried screaming, but her voice suddenly went dry. One silhouette pinned her down to the ground, one silhouette yanked her legs wide and held them still, one silhouette pulled out a knife and lowered it between her legs.

Helpless, Chipiwa gave in to the spirited intents of the three dark savages. She winced in pain as she felt the sharp blade of the knife cut at the delicateness between her legs. It cut and cut and cut. Until she felt no more pain, just a feeling of wetness around her pelvis which she knew was her blood. She had no idea when the horror cutting ended; she only remembered waking up in the morning with a jerk. She felt something unusually sticky between her legs. Curiously, she reached down there with her hand and brought it up to her eyes.

Chipiwa screamed. Blood. Her fingertips had blood on them. This was no longer a nightmare, but reality. Panicking, Chipiwa untangled herself from the blanket and quickly got up from the floor, wondering how she had got there. She went to stand by the window, which was generously letting the morning light in, thanks to the thin, lacy curtain that had been on it since the advent of time. She held up her dress and looked. It was real blood.

Her grandmother suddenly barged into the room just when she was about to make another scream.

"What is all that screaming about, Chipiwa?" her grandmother queried, but Chipiwa needn't have answered. Her grandmother saw the raised dress and lowered her gaze down to her legs. She saw it but didn't look scared. In fact, Chipiwa thought she saw a glow of relief on her grandmother's countenance. This troubled her.

"Nothing to scream about. You are now a woman, Chipiwa." her grandmother said, with what looked like a smile on her face. "Go and bath, nicely. And I will teach you how to take care of yourself during your days."

Chipiwa went out to the outdoor lavatory near the mulberry tree at the back of the house and filled a pail with water from the tap which always had a muddy, khaki colour in the morning. She stood by the tap, leaning against the wall of the lavatory, waiting for Dhuke, her grandmother's tenant who lived in the small outside room which was meant to be the kitchen, to finish whatever he was doing behind the tightly closed door of the toilet. When he finally came out pulling together his trousers and buckling up his belt, Chipiwa stood with her legs tightly held together and looked away. She didn't want Dhuke to see what had happened to her or he would start asking endless questions in his quivering, annoying voice.

She quietly slipped into the lavatory and washed herself in the cold water with a piece of green soap she found in the soapbox. She thought she felt a pain in her lower abdomen, but it was slight and not as terrible as the pain from the lacerations of that bloodthirsty knife from the nightmare. Suddenly, she remembered the nightmare. Did it have anything to do with the uncomfortable experience she had just woken up to? Surely it did, and she wondered if she should tell her grandmother about it. But then, she hadn't told her grandmother when something like that had happened to her before. Maybe because it wasn't a nightmare. It had happened to her while she was fully awake, in full daylight. Not once, not twice, but many times. Maybe because the person who had done to her was not some dark, anonymous silhouette but someone with a real face, someone she saw every day. Maybe she hadn't told her grandmother because she had been told that she was a trustworthy girl who wouldn't say anything about it to anyone. Maybe because it wasn't necessarily an attack. Just friendly play. But now, in retrospect, the thing felt like an attack, just like the attack in the nightmare.

The first time it happened was on a Saturday afternoon. She had gone to Mai Gezimati's house to collect more pieces of lace to make dresses for her dolls. She had been invited by the tailor to come and help herself to as many lace cuttings as she could handle. Mai Gezimati had seen her picking up pieces of lace that had fallen off the sewing table at Tsiga Store. Saturdays she worked from home. Sundays was when she attended to the hordes of people that came to her home seeking her divine services. Apart from being a well-known dressmaker, Mai Gezimati was also a helper and seer. She could see calamities before they happened and advise people on remedies to take and she could treat any kind of problem caused by evil spirits.

She lived alone in the small three roomed house that was next to Chipiwa's. Her husband was a truck driver who was home only twice or thrice a year. Chipiwa had never seen him, only his long truck which he parked in the street, blocking the front view of six houses on the street for at least two days.

She was sitting on the sofa in the sitting room when Chipiwa arrived.

"Come inside, Chipiwa, when you have got what you want," she had told Chipiwa in a tone that made her sound like she was Chipiwa's agemate. Chipiwa picked up a few more strips of lace scattered under the sewing table on the veranda, stuffed them into the bulging empty bread bag she had brought along and went inside.

The woman was too friendly that day, making Chipiwa feel uneasy. Sensing her uneasiness, she came to sit closer to her. Chipiwa could smell the overwhelming waft of something like gumtrees emanating from the woman's body. Chipiwa recognised the smell as the ointment she gave to people, including her grandmother, which had the power to drive away *zvidhoma* and evil spirits.

She chatted to Chipiwa in the same cheesy tone.

"What Grade are you now?"

"Seven."

"Grown woman, ehh. Your father wouldn't recognise you if he were to be deported home from South Africa today. Would you still recognise him?"

Head shake.

"Do you miss him?"

"No."

"Who is your friend at school?"

Shrug of shoulders.

"You prefer playing with your dolls?"

"Yes."

"How many dolls do you have?"

"Many."

She asked some more questions about Chipiwa's dolls. Before the touching started. It started just like friendly caresses on the hand, neck, thigh, stomach. Then, when they spread to places more private, places that made Chipiwa feel more guilty, the touches became more intense and aggressive.

It was just play, Chipiwa was told. Play between two friends, and she knew Chipiwa wasn't going to tell anyone about it, she had said, because Chipiwa was a good girl just like her dolls that didn't complain or badmouth her.

The touching went on for numerous Saturdays, and Chipiwa was given more lace trimmings to take home at the end of each visit.

When she returned to the house after taking the bath, she found her grandmother sitting on the sofa, next to the mound of her blankets strewn about the sofa, Tate in her hands, turning the doll over and over suspiciously like it were some sort of talisman she had just stumbled upon. Chipiwa's heart sank.

"What is this, Chipiwa?"

Chipiwa didn't answer. She knew it was rhetoric, and when her grandmother asks rhetoric, trouble was a moment away.

"Did I not say no more dolls?"

Chipiwa didn't answer. She felt an itch on the calf of her leg but remained still.

"Look at you, a grown-up woman, still playing with dolls! A shame. You are such a shame."

***

Tete Rubhiya came exactly one week after Chipiwa's blood days had ended. She found Chipiwa serving a *fodya* customer by the gate. She marveled at how grown up Chipiwa looked, said something about Chipiwa's bourgeoning chest before going into the house where her grandmother was. Tete Rubhiya was grandmother's eldest child, but whenever she was here, she spoke with so much authority in her voice you would think she was grandmother's mother instead.

Chipiwa didn't like Tete Rubhiya. She hated the bright and shiny dresses she wore that made her look like a giant crayon, but more importantly, she hated the way she spoke about her father, whom she referred to as "your *mampara baba*" when talking to Chipiwa, and "that useless boy of yours," when talking to grandmother.

"She is now at a dangerous stage. It's important you keep a keen eye on her," Tete Rubhiya was saying when Chipiwa got into the house holding a dirty one dollar note.

Her grandmother mumbled something in response, something about the good for nothing boys from Majubheki.

"It's not only the boys, mother. Even the men. Real grown men are the most dangerous. You should have seen where the eyes of that *mdhara* pretending to buy *fodya* at the gate were all the time; on her breasts!" Tete Rubhiya said, without giving any regard to Chipiwa's presence.

"You should check her. From time to time. Just to make sure," she added with emphasis.

"Check her?" grandmother quizzed with narrowed eyes and a furrowed forehead.

"Yes, check her. To see if she's still OK."

Her grandmother exhaled heavily, slowly nodded her head and looked at Chipiwa.

***

"What do you mean she is not whole?" Chipiwa clearly heard her grandmother's trouble-laced voice from the sitting room. She had remained behind in her grandmother's bedroom after Tete Rubhiya had burst out of the room in a fit of bubbling anger following the "checking".

Tete Rubhiya had explained to Chipiwa how what she was doing was good for her impending womanhood. She would continue doing what she was about to do from time to time, all in the interest of preserving her womanhood.

After the explaining, she made Chipiwa take off her pant and asked her to "sit on the bed like this, with your legs like this... No, not like that... like this, yes."

And then she touched her.

"I checked her, she is not whole!" Tete Rubhiya shouted out the anger in her voice, like someone spitting out a hot chilli.

"How come she is not whole?" Grandmother's voice was improbably calm yet edged in a fearful intonation.

"I don't know! You tell me how come; you live with her!"

Grandmother was silent for a moment, then, "She will tell me. She will tell me!"

Chipiwa heard the front door pushed open noisily, heard her grandmother's footsteps on the veranda outside, heard the snapping sound of a thick switch being broken from the mulberry tree, heard the sound of leaves being plucked off it in one continuous whoosh, then heard her grandmother's footsteps walk back into the house.

Chipiwa silently moved to the window, pushed it open, jumped out. And went quietly.

Salma Amanda Latifa

Salma Amanda Latifa is an avid reader and writer with a deep love for literature. She finds joy in exploring books from various genres, especially romance, comedy, and mystery. Her passion for storytelling is evident in her admiration for the works of Arthur Conan Doyle and J.K. Rowling, making her a devoted fan of Sherlock Holmes and Harry Potter. Beyond books, Salma enjoys relaxing by watching romantic comedy films from the early 2000s, relishing the light-hearted and feel-good nature of these movies.

Nana and the New Neighbour
Salma Amanda Latifa – Egypt

In a small town, there lived a young girl named Nana. Nana always woke up earlier than her pet chicken named Kiky. The reason she woke up earlier than the chicken was because Kiky would always give a "concert" with its crowing under Nana's window, startling her half to death every morning. However, this morning, Nana had a plan for revenge to surprise Kiky.

Initially, Nana considered the idea of cooking Kiky as chicken soup as a form of revenge for the morning concert that often startled her. However, this desire was hindered by a sudden reluctance that arose in Nana's heart. This was because Kiky had once given her a memorable birthday surprise, a moment still fresh in her memory. Remembering that surprise could bring a smile to Nana's face, and her affection for Kiky made her hesitate to carry out the plan.

However, Nana's life became more enjoyable that morning when a new family appeared behind her house, bringing along a handsome young boy. Nana often saw him busy in the guava tree behind the house, his eyes always shining brightly as he watered the flowers with enthusiasm.

But there was one problem: Nana had no idea what the name of the handsome boy who made her heartbeat faster was. One day, Nana decided to uncover this mystery and started exploring the neighbourhood in the hope that the handsome figure would suddenly appear before her.

Suddenly, her friend named Kevin appeared in front of her, complete with his mischievous smile. "Hey, Nana! Have you met the new neighbour?" Kevin asked with a squint in his eyes. He knew that Nana liked the new neighbour because her joy was always evident whenever she talked about him.

Nana just grinned, and with a shy face, she said, "Not yet, Kevin. I want to, but I don't know how."

Kevin, who always liked to joke around, immediately suggested a crazy idea, "Come on, let's call him Jolly Jake! To give it an artistic impression." Nana chuckled hearing Kevin's suggestion.

"Jolly Jake, huh? It's a weird idea, but why not?" she replied with a smile.

They both started developing a plan to introduce themselves to the new neighbour, and at the same time, to ensure Nana's love story went smoothly. They decided to make a simple gift for the handsome guy, a bouquet of flowers they took from Nana's backyard. Kevin also suggested making a greeting card with sweet and cheerful handwritten notes.

After preparing their gift, Nana and Kevin went to the new neighbour's house. They walked with enthusiasm, discussing strategies to make a good impression on the handsome guy. When they arrived at his house, they saw him cleaning the front yard.

The handsome guy looked at Nana and Kevin with surprise as they approached him. Nana tried to contain her nervousness and with a broad smile, she greeted, "Hi, Jolly Jake! We, Nana and Kevin, are your neighbours. We brought a small gift for you as a welcome gesture to our neighbourhood!"

Jolly Jake smiled warmly and accepted their gift. He opened the greeting card made by Nana and Kevin, laughing cheerfully as he read the sweet handwritten notes. "Thank you, both of you! Jolly Jake? That's a unique name, but I like it! Thanks again, Nana and Kevin."

Nana, still nervous, tried to lighten the mood with a joke, "Oh, and we decided to give you that name because we thought it would make life here more colourful!"

Kevin added with a serious tone, "And of course, because we're very artistic."

Jolly Jake laughed and nodded in agreement. "Alright, Jolly Jake it is! Thanks, guys. I'm glad to have friendly neighbours like you, and by the way, my real name is Alex."

Nana and Kevin exchanged confused glances. It turned out the nickname "Jolly Jake" they had given was far from the reality of the handsome guy's actual name. They tried to hide their confusion, and casually, Kevin said, "Oh, of course, Alex! We just gave you a stage name for a more impressive touch, right?"

Nana chimed in, "Yeah, Kevin thought Jolly Jake sounded better, but Alex is the name I prefer!"

Alex just smiled and nodded understandingly. "Alright, Jolly Jake or

Alex, you can call me either. But hey, thanks again for the warm welcome."

They chatted for a while, but suddenly, a loud crowing sound was heard from behind them. Kiky, Nana's pet chicken, had escaped from its coop and was wandering in Alex's front yard. Nana panicked and shouted, "Kiky! Don't disrupt this meeting!"

Nana quickly ran towards Kiky, who was busy exploring the front yard. They all looked, surprised at this small commotion, while Nana tried to calm the situation. "Sorry, it seems Kiky slipped out of his coop. I'll get him right away," Nana said with a slightly embarrassed smile.

Nana managed to catch Kiky after a few attempts and brought it back to the coop. She returned to the meeting with a somewhat flushed face, trying to restore the atmosphere.

"Our meeting feels livelier with that incident, doesn't it?" Alex said with a smile. Nana just nodded shyly, and Kevin chuckled softly at the earlier event. They continued their conversation, this time with louder laughter accompanying them.

After the funny incident with Kiky the day before, the friendship between Nana, Kevin, and Alex became even closer. They shared stories about daily life, laughed together, and planned activities together in their neighbourhood.

Alex turned out to have a talent for gardening, and Nana, who also enjoyed gardening, was delighted to receive tips and tricks from Alex. Kevin, who wasn't initially interested in gardening, joined in to experience their joy. They began forming a small community focused on communal activities and a shared love for the environment.

Not long after, they planned a community garden event in Nana's backyard. All the neighbours were invited to share gardening knowledge, exchange seedlings, and even participate in a competition for the best garden. The event became a fun moment that strengthened the relationships among the residents in their neighbourhood.

During this time, Nana began to feel that her feelings for Alex were growing. Their closeness made Nana more comfortable and happier. However, she hesitated to express her feelings, fearing it might ruin the friendship that had developed in the past few days.

One day, as they sat on the front porch of Nana's house, Nana finally confessed her feelings to Alex. "Alex, since the moment I first saw you, I felt that my life became more colourful and enjoyable. I like you, Alex," Nana said with a hopeful expression.

Alex was momentarily surprised but then smiled and responded, "Nana, I feel the same way. I'm glad to have a friend like you, but I have to be honest with you; right now I'm not ready for a romantic relationship. I value our friendship, and I'm worried that taking it further might change the dynamic between the three of us," Alex said gently.

Nana felt disappointed, but she tried to keep smiling. "I appreciate your honesty, Alex. Our friendship means a lot to me, and I don't want this decision to ruin our relationship."

Alex nodded, "Thank you for understanding, Nana. I hope we can still be good friends like we are now."

They smiled at each other, although the atmosphere became a bit awkward. Kevin, who had always been the mediator of their joy, tried to ease the tension with his humour, "Hey, Nana, maybe this is a sign for us to embark on a new adventure as a brave trio who always supports each other!"

Nana chuckled at Kevin's words, and the atmosphere became cheerful again, albeit with a changed dynamic. Alex added, "Kevin is right, we can still have a strong relationship as friends. I hope we can continue our fun activities together."

After that slightly tense moment, they continued their activities as usual. The community garden event was a success, albeit with a different vibe. They continued to support each other and share happiness, creating beautiful memories that adorned their lives in the small town.

That night, after the successful community garden event, Nana, Kevin, and Alex decided to spend time together on Nana's front porch. They sat on folding chairs with a cup of warm tea, enjoying the tranquillity of the quiet night.

Nana gazed at the stars in the sky and said, "Even though it's not what I imagined, I'm glad to have both of you as friends."

Kevin nodded in agreement, "Absolutely, Nana. Sometimes, friendships can be stronger and more enduring. And who knows what will happen in the future, right?"

Alex added, "We may not know what the future holds, but I'm truly grateful to have both of you in my life. We can continue enjoying our fun activities and supporting each other."

They fell silent for a moment, enjoying the quiet night filled with the rustling sounds of leaves in the wind. The warm atmosphere of their friendship brought peace to each of their hearts.

"Alright, enough with the serious talk," Kevin said with a mischievous smile. "Any ideas for our next activity?"

Nana chuckled, "Hmm, maybe we could have a picnic in the park tomorrow, and this time, let's make sure Kiky doesn't interfere with our meeting."

Everyone agreed with Nana's idea, and they began planning the picnic for the next day. With laughter, jokes, and exciting plans, the night ended with overflowing happiness. Life continued in their small town, filled with adventures and joy.

The next morning, they prepared for the picnic in the park. Kiky, seemingly eager to be part of the activity, gave a supportive crow as Nana, Kevin, and Alex headed to the park, ready to embrace a day full of joy together. And so, their friendship story in this beautiful small town continued.

Augustine Tashinga Mudzudza

Augustine Tashinga Mudzudza is a Zimbabwean law student and content creator. He is a chronically online nerd who reviews books on his Youtube channel, 'Augustine T' and shares his favourite books on his Instagram @its_august_ine. He also runs a X (formerly Twitter) account under the same name and blogs about a wide range of issues on byaugustine.wordpress.com. He's a competitive speaker in the African debate circuit and was a semi-finalist at the 2024 Southern African Universities Debate Championship.

Where The Heart Is
Augustine Tashinga Mudzudza – Zimbabwe

As the plane touched down, Yevedzo felt a familiar tension gripping her body, making it stiffen and press itself against her seat.

"Mum, you're making that face again," Bonnie said, sipping her Capri-Sun.

"What face, love?"

"The one you make when something's not quite right."

"I'm fine, just a little excited for you to see where I grew up," Yevedzo said, forcing a weak smile. Bonnie was not convinced, but she did not ask further. Yevedzo did not look excited. And she was certainly not fine either.

She could not remember when she had started doubting herself again, but she was stuck, rethinking yet another major decision. It must have started the moment she purchased the flight tickets. No. It was from when she jolted awake one night, sweating, panting and consumed by an overwhelming nostalgia. Or perhaps it was during her first encounter with her Scottish neighbour in Durham.

She had just moved from London and the neighbour had pestered her about where she was *really* from, refusing to believe that she had just moved from London because the rent was now too high. To the rotund woman with a grey mole on her chin, Yevedzo had to have moved from somewhere like the Congo, because the wars were too bad, or from someplace she insisted was called 'Zimbabi', because the prices of bread were too high. The woman's dense face had lit up in glee when Yevedzo told her she had, in fact, emigrated from Zimbabwe. But Yevedzo had pronounced it wrong. The country's name was pronounced 'Zimbabi', not Zimbabwe and the Scottish woman was certain *her* pronunciation was right, her reason being that she had a best friend whose aunt's godmother had been on holiday to Victoria Falls before she died – back when the nation was called Rhodesia, when the country was still worth something, when bread did not cost so much.

It struck her for the first time during that moment that Bonnie knew just as little of Zimbabwe as this woman did.

Yevedzo's excuses to keep her roots buried away had successively surfaced and dismissed themselves in her mind. *The trip would be expensive! Nobody would remember or recognise her. Bonnie would not have a good time.* But none of those reasons mattered anymore now that the plane's wheels rested gracefully on Zimbabwean tarmac. They were useless now that her daughter's curious eyes shot from aisle to window and to aisle again, her lips sucking hungrily on her Capri-Sun, which crumpled more and more with each sip, as if she was trying to savour every last bit of the United Kingdom she had brought with her before allowing her feet to become acquainted with Zimbabwean soil for the very first time. At last, she took the packet from her lips, wrinkled and empty, carrying an aged emptiness that echoed the one which drove Yevedzo to make this decision, to visit home.

***

On the drive from the airport to Tariro's home in Glaudina, Yevedzo occasionally looked out of the window, taking in the view of Harare in the waning sunlight. As the radio softly played an effusive gospel medley, the sunset cast an ethereal glow over the landscape, drenching the scene in brilliant golden, amethyst and carnelian hues.

"You know you didn't have to trouble yourself, Tarie."

"Nonsense!" Tariro replied from the driver's seat of her battered Honda Fit, which had a damp smell you could not quite place and whose faux-leather seat covers had worn threadbare with use. "What kind of friend would I be had I let you haggle your way from that shitty airport to an overpriced hotel room?"

"I'd be worse off, that's for sure. You know, I heard you can't even trust taxi drivers anymore."

"My mother's child, is that what you're still asking me at this point? Was it not last week when a pregnant woman's body was found torn open by the highway?" Tariro paused, swerving the car into her neighbourhood.

"Don't tell me!" Yevedzo said, but Tariro went on.

"Ah, friend, people are doing rituals and sacrifices, seeking money when what they really should be seeking is God."

Yevedzo chuckled.

"And you are still your heretical self. But where would we be today without God's hand? I have seen his miracles in my own life."

"I know. But our country needs people who invest as much energy in practical development as they do in prayer. There are some things we simply cannot pray away, Tari. People don't seem to want to work anymore. I even heard stories of people selling their toes for money! Some people would rather disfigure themselves than work."

"Work?" Tariro said, annoyed. "As Zimbabweans, all we ever seem to do is work. You must have forgotten that things here are not the same as they are in England. Here, those people will lie and steal and milk you dry. Even the sweat on your brow will be used to quench those people's thirst."

Yevedzo did not ask who 'those people' were. She knew exactly who they were. Everyone did. They had ransacked the country. They had fattened themselves up on its gold, crops and foreign aid. Their round, smiling faces were plastered on electoral posters throughout the CBD. They had eyes and ears everywhere. They saw everything, heard everything.

Bonnie slept soundly in the backseat of the car as the choral voices from the radio sang, "*Tichadaidza Mwari vedu*. We shall call unto our God."

"So, any word from Brandon?" Tariro asked.

Yevedzo turned to look outside the window as if she had not heard Tariro's question, as if the weeks' worth of uncollected rubbish on the street had suddenly become the most interesting thing to look at.

The silence Tariro got from her friend gave her the answer. Brandon had not reached out. Tariro could tell that Yevedzo was still as heartbroken as she was when she and Brandon stopped talking, when she packed up and left all those years ago.

"So tell me, is it true that you have been wiping the bums of old white women for the past seven years in England?" Tariro said, venturing into safer territory.

"No, that's not all I had to do. I also had the privilege of cleaning their noses and painting their nails, which I thoroughly enjoyed."

They both erupted into peals of laughter which dissolved the tension that had begun to brew, just as easily as it surfaced.

"You know, some people actually think that's what you've been doing."

"I'd better give you a hard drive so you can load all the stories they've been telling about me. I thought I was a lawyer in the UK for all these years."

"Well, the streets beg to differ."

The playful banter went on between them as if they were retired war veterans with many tales to tell, until the car's engine finally stopped humming in Tariro's front yard.

That night, as Yevedzo lay in the guest bedroom of her best friend's house, it was not her village that she thought of, but her sleepless nights in England. She wondered if she had really felt that yearning for home or if she had just imagined it. Her fear of confronting what had happened in the year leading up to Bonnie's birth now outweighed her longing for home. She was no longer certain what home even was. The gaudy "Welcome to Zimbabwe" sign, the churches that lined every street, the streetlights in disrepair plastered with penis enlargement posters, the rotting trees by the roadside, pungent with blood-orange urine; none of it had felt like home. Perhaps the company of her family in the village would. She wrestled with her thoughts in the torrid summer air before finally landing on the tenuous passage that lay between sleep and consciousness.

The bus ride to Nyanga the following morning was chaotic at best. Yevedzo and Bonnie had settled in the middle of the Luxury-City bus, Yevedzo on the aisle and Bonnie on the window seat – she had called dibs. Yevedzo laughed for a second, thinking of how she, as a child, would have never imagined telling her parents not to sit in a spot she wanted for herself.

From the outside, the bus had looked like something out of a comic sketch. Perhaps it was the peeling, faded paint in mismatched colours that read, "Luxury City Luxury Coaches: The ultimate luxury". Although the bus was a mobile red flag, Yevedzo managed to convince herself that all she needed was to get home, no matter the means – this *was* the last morning bus to Nyanga, after all.

The seats felt hard and hollowed out. Yevedzo imagined the bony backsides of thousands of people plopping onto and digging into them, as if expecting to find the gold that disappeared from the country's reserves every other week. They were uneven and firm, with the feel of planks wrapped in satin.

There were three small televisions in the bus, but only one, the one at the very front, seemed to be working. The curtains on the windows were caked with years of dirt and grime. Bonnie was horrified.

Tariro had told Yevedzo to be safe. It was Remembrance Day after all, and people often went wild on holidays. She had told her friend she would be safe. But what threatened her safety on that particular ride was beyond the scope of her imagination.

The rude conductor had already collected everybody's fares when it started. A number of hawkers had stormed the bus, selling everything from prescription drugs to deep-fried birds. Some even tried to sell toothbrushes, which they desperately needed themselves. The bus had passed a few towns, and the same gospel music video was playing on loop on the grainy television. Yevedzo's earphones were plugged in her ears when she felt Bonnie tightly gripping her arm. Yanking them off, she turned to face her daughter – and she felt the entire bus turning with her.

"Mummy!" Bonnie yelled as the bus made a sharp turn, speeding off the road and into the veld. When it finally made a jolt as the driver hit the brakes, throwing the passengers up from their seats, Yevedzo clutched her daughter tightly in her arms as screams filled the vehicle.

"Mama look, look at the road!" a small voice screamed before an older one reprimanded it for yelling and pointing at things in public. That, however, did not stop people from seeing.

On the highway, right in the middle where the white lines separated the lanes, a procession of cars adorned with tiny national flags on their bonnets blazed past. The cars looked mean and menacing as they claimed dominance, ownership over the entire road.

A chorus of angry voices questioned why a godsent ruler would travel in such a manner, endangering the lives of civilians, before one gruff voice told them to leave and start their own countries. The voice belonged to a toothless old man in the backseat, who was drowning in a pastel blazer held together by shoddy patchwork. In Yevedzo's mind, it made more sense for men like him, who had lived through war and shattered dreams, to be angry about leaders who built roads for their people just to push them off.

She began to feel a numbness, a sadness, a hopelessness she had not felt in a very long time. It was the very one that had driven her away from this country, from what she had always perceived as home. Bonnie was shaking and she could see that same hopelessness etched on the faces of the people seated across from her. It lingered in the folds of the drooping flesh of the emaciated cattle grazing dolefully by the roadside. It was ingrained in the filthy curtains on the bus, and it abounded in the thick, unwashed armpit stench that enveloped the bus.

The music video continued to play mockingly, almost cruelly, "…Ebenezer, God you have brought us here…" When the bus finally came to life again, it did not seem to spring with as much vigour as it had back in Mbare. It felt like it carried the very disillusionment that weighed the people's hearts down. As it carried on, a mournful silence ensued between Yevedzo and Bonnie, before she asked, "What just happened mum?" her eyes tinged with a vexed sadness.

Yevedzo had barely come up with an answer when the bus came screeching and moaning to a halt. *Had it broken down? Was it out of fuel?*

As she looked over Bonnie's head, out of the window, she gasped and quickly told her to cover her eyes.

"What is happening, mum?" Bonnie asked, her voice breaking and tears starting to pool in her eyes. Yevedzo was at a loss for words. She felt regretful about having come back. Getting no response from her mother, Bonnie opened her eyes and horror spread across her face.

The scene outside told a story. It was not a happy one. Three vehicles; a hatchback, a small truck and an omnibus, had sped off the road and were now huddled in a heartbreaking embrace. There were three bodies lying lifeless beside the steaming mess. A small group of people sat close together in the sweltering sun, and an angry man with a crimson cut across his arm was screaming heatedly into a cell phone. These people had not been lucky.

Other drivers had stopped too. They had parked their pretty cars next to the mangled ones and now stood gawking at the accident scene and taking pictures, documenting the victims' misery. The pictures would probably end up on Facebook, captioned "Zimbabwean Lives Matter", with comments of sympathy from angry diasporans sipping chocolate milk in countries that would never be theirs. The sad part was, not even their home country had felt like their own.

It was them, the ones with plastic banana smiles, the perpetually pregnant men whose mean cars had sped along the highway – they had caused this.

Yevedzo wondered what lay ahead. If the day's events held a deeper meaning, they certainly did not augur well. She could not begin to imagine what waited for her back home, on the homestead where she had grown up.

***

Yevedzo woke up to the sound of little voices bouncing around the homestead before her eyes took in the thatch ceiling of the small hut she had spent the night in. It was the same one she had spent her childhood in with her two sisters, one now late, the other married to a Muslim man and whose sons' names began with Abdul.

Of all the voices in the yard, Bonnie's was distinct, with its foreign accent that distorted every Shona word she said. It sounded bold and bright, different from how it had when they had gotten here a few days prior. On the night they had arrived, walking into the homestead in the pale moonlight, with the goats' eyes flashing like radioactive sequins, Bonnie remained silent and zombie-eyed, failing to find home in this hopeless place.

Now, her voice appeared confident, melting into the ruckus of juvenile chaos.

It was not until a sharp scream tore through the morning air that Yevedzo jolted from her reed mat and cocked her head towards the direction it had come from. *Was that Bonnie?*

Tying a long cloth across her torso, she dashed out of the hut and saw three things that were taking place. There was a rooster chasing a hen around the compound. There were children standing in a circle, jeering at someone in the middle. Then there was the little girl at the centre of the circle with tears streaming down her face, her mouth wide open and runny mucus dripping from her nose.

Yevedzo got a stick from a nearby tree and brandished it at the children, yelling at them to go away. Some ran to their mothers' huts while others went a short distance, only far enough away to laugh at both Yevedzo and Bonnie without getting hit.

85

As she approached Bonnie, Yevedzo noticed a thin, crimson line running down her arm. Before she could ask what had happened, Tambudzayi, an old, sickly woman who seemed to appear from nowhere began, "Your child must know her place. Who does she think she is, playing with roosters?"

Yevedzo sent a querying look at her daughter, who narrated amidst tears, sniffles and hiccups, how she had tried to rescue a hen from a mean rooster.

The old woman's jaw fell apart before she made throaty, guttural sounds. Her face was weirdly contorted. She looked like she was in pain, but she was laughing hysterically.

Yevedzo looked around and saw the rooster harassing a fat brown hen. The hen was big, but the cock was bigger. The rooster's beak, the same one that had pecked at Bonnie's arm without hesitation, was now clenched around the neck of that brown hen. Its body was moving rapidly on top of the hen's, whose feathers flapped hopelessly in vain protest, before the rooster finally let the hen go and the two birds began to walk idly beside each other, like two old friends making small talk.

By this time, mothers had been dragged out of their kitchens by their children to see the 'salad woman' from England, whose silly daughter had tried to fight a bird.

"You'd think these people, with their good English and nasal accent, would have more sense. *Mashura chaiwo!*" one of the women said, before the old woman snapped at her, reminding her who had brought the huge hamper of groceries in her kitchen.

"Your lover is coming today," the old woman said, watching Yevedzo closely.

"What does he want? I came here to see you, Mother. Not some man who abandoned me and still hasn't said a word. Our lives could've been perfect together. We would've built a nice home, the two of us, if he hadn't chosen that path."

"You know people don't choose those things, my child. The spirit picks whomever it wants."

"You don't understand, Mhamha, that I had to bear a burden because of that. People I had called my friends gossiped and called me a whore when I didn't discover I was pregnant until after I went *ku*UK."

By this time, Bonnie had moved to a nearby tree and was ripping pieces of bark off the trunk. This girl with sand in her hair and mud plastered on her dress and mucus dried on her face and tears dried on her cheeks, did not look like the one who had been excited to go on holiday to Africa.

"And yet you did not have to do any of that in the first place! You should've come here, to the village where you belong, and you would've honoured your ancestors," Tambudzayi said.

"Stayed here? And become a witch doctor's wife? Me, a woman with a law degree giving up so many opportunities just to settle down with a man who likes to play with herbs? No. Brandon was okay with *that* lifestyle, but not me."

"Your husband gave up his career. He gave you up, he kissed his life goodbye to honour his duty. Nobody ever just does that. Brandon is coming to see you today whether you like it or not. And shouldn't you be nursing your daughter's wound?" Tambudzayi said, before hobbling off to her hut.

Yevedzo walked up to Bonnie and lifted her into her arms, and she was gripped by an overwhelming panic.

"Mum you're making that face again," Bonnie said, her eyes reddened by tears.

"Don't worry about me, love," Yevedzo said, her feet raising little clouds of red dust as she walked back to her hut.

After Bonnie had been cleaned up, she ran back to the other children. This time, they were playing house.

Yevedzo found herself picking out a floral dress, plaiting her hair and rehearsing a series of greetings in her head. She could not believe that a man she had loathed for seven years still made her nervous, still made her want to look her best. Maybe she had not actually hated him at all.

At midday, as she sat in her hut, Bonnie now fast asleep on a small reed mat, Yevedzo heard a booming voice echoing from the gates of the compound and she felt her breath hitch. She could hear her heartbeat pounding in her ears, which were heating up more and more with each passing second. She heard Tambudzayi welcoming the voice into the compound. Yevedzo knew that voice. It was *his* voice.

They had been separated by custom, by duty. Perhaps speaking to him again and looking into his eyes once more would feel like home.

She rubbed her sweaty palms on her dress before she stood up. She was probably making that face. She heard someone knock on her door three times.

It was him.

She opened the door and was met with the judgmental eyes that had watched her throughout her childhood.

It was not him.

"You are nervous," Tambudzayi said as she stood in the doorway, seeing the look on her daughter's face. A brief silence ensued between them. "Well, it is time. You better not keep him waiting."

"But he didn't mind making me wait all these yea—"

Tambudzayi hugged her child, stopping her mid-sentence.

"I know, my child. You have been fighting all these years. Sometimes, you do not have to fight the people you love."

Love. That was it. She still loved him. It was the only reason for coming back that actually felt true.

Tambudzayi kissed her daughter's face and left the hut.

Left to get ready, Yevedzo turned around and wiped a tear on the right side of her face, a tear she had not even known was there.

She walked over to Bonnie and gently woke her up. As Bonnie slowly blinked away the sleep in her eyes, she could only vaguely hear Yevedzo's voice. She was making that face again.

"Bonnie, let's go meet your father."

Chioniso Tsikisayi

Chioniso Tsikisayi is a writer, NAMA nominated poet, filmmaker and playwright from Bulawayo, Zimbabwe. She was first runner up for the 65th Kenya Poetry Slam Africa Contest. Her work has been featured in Brittle Paper, Isele Magazine, The Kalahari Review, Ipikai Poetry Journal, Agbowó, AFREADA, Lolwe, Intwasa Short Stories Volume Two, Imbiza Journal for African Writing, Tesserae; a mosaic of poems by Zimbabwean women. In 2022, her debut play, 'A Woman Has Two Mouths' was shortlisted for the African Women Playwrights Network Festival of Plays held in Accra, Ghana. She won the Canopus Award 2023 for excellence in interstellar writing in the Original Local Short Form Fiction Category for her short story "Gumbojena." She won the Ibua Bold Continental Call for Climate Change, Poetry category and the 2023 Roil Bulawayo Arts Award for Outstanding Poet of the Year. She is a Creative Writing Alumni of the Johannesburg Institute for Advanced Study. Her debut novel 'What It Means To Outlive A Daughter' was longlisted for the 2024 Island Prize.

The Beautiful Sound of Water
Chioniso Tsikisayi – Zimbabwe

2 Chronicles 7:14
If my people, who are called by my name, will humble themselves and pray and seek my face and turn from their wicked ways, then I will forgive their sins and heal their land.

There is no water.
It is hot,
again.
On days like this, the earth is a woman begging for a kiss of rain, but Heaven will not touch her parched lips. Heaven will not make love to her, the kind of love that brews into a gentle, thundering storm. The kind of love that showers a spouse, cleansing and intimate. Forgiving. I miss the rain. I miss the smell of wet earth, and the salt in red anthills whose soil pregnant women sometimes eat. I crave it, now.

I think of those lonely, wet days in November after school, my head pressed against a window in a noisy ZUPCO bus commuting home, watching jewels of water stain the glass like sparkling teardrops. And the delicious, smoky aroma of mealies roasted on the roadside still wrapped in their husks, still warm, lingering in a passenger's handbag. The whistle of traffic and the crunch of gravel under car tires. People navigating the damp streets in old raincoats with bread or newspapers tucked under the arm. Others leaving work with their perms concealed beneath plastic shopping bags serving as shower caps. Secretaries, cleaners, waiters, shopkeepers. Civilian life unfolding within the mechanics of existing, oblivious to the homeless picking out scraps of food from restaurant refuse, all while the skies continued weeping like a song.

I miss the sweetness of its scent. The coolness of the night air; how lovely it felt against the skin. Those evenings we placed buckets outside, singing and collecting stones in metal tins. Our mothers hanging laundry to dry in the living room, our fathers smoking cigarettes on the street corners and music from the bottle stores spilling out of cars. *Ishwa* flying in a dizzied frenzy around the light bulbs, catching them, roasting them till the bottoms were golden brown…

Spider sneaks off to the corner of the house, a cloud of flies hanging on to his tail like a funeral procession. He doesn't bark anymore.

"Come on, boy." His one good eye slowly trails my hand. I throw him a piece of sadza and he laps it up quickly. The bones beneath his jet-black fur protrude like spokes in a bicycle.

The drought is five years old now. It is a toddler, still nursing at the breast of our affliction. We are at the mercy of its silent tantrums, unable to wean it off the cracked nipple of our malnourished prayers.

It is 1995.

My name is Mpilo.

My mother was murdered in the massacres. The one no one speaks of. We do not yet have a language to name the loss, to qualify the grief, but we have inherited its scars like ornaments. Ancient artefacts of terror. The cords of trauma that bind us…

This is the legacy of pain.

The drought has ushered me through adolescence, through the crimson cycles of my blood and the dry spells in between. The geography of my body has changed while it has remained constant. I have become the shape of a woman, twenty-one years young, curves and flesh splattered with stretch marks, hips that swivel like the walls of Kariba Dam. It is my mother's beauty that I have inherited. Her peaks and valleys hewn out of the granite boulders of Matobo Hills.

Although I am the shape of a woman, I am hollow; possessing the feminine form but not knowing its full power.

"It's time to bring the cows home to your father." Amai's older sister has noticed the changes. We live together in the compound. She has witnessed me blossom like clustered grapefruit, ripe for marriage, specially picked from the bridal tree.

"Follow the customs, bring blessings upon your family through obedience. This is the duty of every woman."

These days water is the currency for which we exchange our lives and bodies like sacrificial pieces on a chess board. The old kitchen tap burps dust from time to time. It coughs like an old man, like one of my uncles who smokes cigarettes religiously. An ancient rusty thing that once was a portal to refreshment. I use the black container outside the house to wash our mugs, plates and spoons. I can't remember the last time my ears were blessed with the beautiful sound of water gurgling in the pipes, a sweet liquid symphony filling the arteries of the vessel that is our home or the music of a toilet flushing without the aid of a bucket.

I wet my washcloth each morning and wipe it across my forehead, shoulders and between my thighs. It's not the same as immersing yourself in water. A full, steaming bath. Feeling clean, skin scrubbed smooth and smelling of soap. When the water cuts first began it would go for days at a time like a wandering lover, and when it returned, it came bearing the filth of unfaithfulness. Undrinkable.

The City Council said we had nothing to worry about. A water rationing schedule had been introduced. Things would soon be normal again. But days turned into weeks and then weeks bled into months of pregnant silence. Like a marriage on the verge of breaking down were the miscarried promises of the government to its people. Only some parts of the city still had water on a weekly basis.

It became a new religion of sorts.

The most elite have commodified water as a luxury, as a sign of affluence and prestige. Business owners, ministers, religious leaders. In the politics of thirst, we relegate ourselves to the most atrocious of things. Time is measured in drops of water. Five o'clock in the mornings, we queue for hours in line to use the solitary squeaky pump near St. Columbus Church. The sun creeps up from out of its bed in the sky and dances on our backs as we struggle with buckets atop our heads, sloshing liquid across the bridge, finding our way home in the scorching heat.

Deep in the greener suburbs of the city where there are homes with lush gardens and boreholes, the crisis of thirst is an illusion.

Bottled water is sold in the shops, clear blue plastic containers of the precious liquid. Often times, when I can afford to get bread, I stare longingly at the 2 litre containers behind the glass of the supermarket refrigerator. What does purified mineral water taste like? Isn't water just water? Or is water segregated into classes like people are? The VIP section and the general public. I wonder if bottled water feels superior to tap water, if tap water feels superior to the sewage that flows under the bridge on Jacaranda Road, a swirling mass of stench and decay that permeates the air with smells of sickness and death.

Some of us fetch water from there. The poorest of us.

My best friend was given away in marriage to a local councillor in exchange for a JoJo Tank. We grew up together in the dusty streets of Magwegwe. Girls with big dreams and bright eyes. We do not speak anymore. She has quietly assimilated into money. All evidence of an impoverished past erased from the spotless profile of a public figure's wife. The ghost of our relationship lingers.

Baba says we are better because we live in town.

By that, he means we are suffering moderately. By that, he means we should be grateful for our portion of misery. How do you think people in the rural areas are surviving? No food for their livestock. Failing crops. Nothing to depend on except for the sporadic handouts of government relief packages on the rare occasion that the country remembers that people in the village are citizens of the nation too.

The NGOs are here too. Supplying grain and medicine. Documenting the sad bits. Every month, there are dead bodies being collected from homes. The lack of access to water leads to a succession of illnesses: cholera, typhoid and dysentery. There are families grieving in black, whose throats are too parched to wail, whose eyes are starved of liquid, and so they do not cry anymore. We watch with a quiet resignation as bodies are placed in metal caskets and thrown into the back of police trucks for those with no funeral policies. Tomorrow it could be either one of us, lying stiffly in oblivion, the blood running cold. It could be either one of us in the back of a pickup.

"When are you getting married?" Baba is like a withered tree sitting in the sun. "That classmate of yours… what's her name? Julia?"

"What about her, Baba?" I ask.

"She bought her father a new house." There is a tone of resentment in his voice.

"That's lovely for her."

"It should have been you."

"I'll get you a house."

"It's not about the house. It's about security," he says. "I won't be around much longer. You need a man, a good one to take care of you."

Baba has not forgiven me for turning down the councillor's proposal. He approached me first before he settled for my best friend.

"It should have been you." It is the song my father sings every day.

But there is someone else I love.

A Lucky Dube record is booming from someone's car stereo next door, and the cool sounds of reggae fill the atmosphere like condensing clouds. It's lunch hour. I sit in the outside shed, cleaning chicken intestines in a small Kango bowl, watching the sky change colour. It's a pale orange, sometimes grey but most times it's nothing. The nothingness that plagues this place. I blow into the hearth. Flames rise to lick the blackened base of the pot, and the oil sings.

There are many things to atone for in this place of slaughter. For those who died ne*shungu*. Maiguru says the rains will not come, not while there is still blood staining the earth's body. She says that all things have memory, trees and rocks and flowers. That the roots of living things feel so deeply. That rivers are not simply rivers but a flowing of God's consciousness. Our identity is in the water.

This is our heritage. Njelele, the rain making shrine, is a sacred place hidden in the spiritual capital Matopos. It is where God's voice could be heard in the past. Where He spoke to his people centuries before my existence. But we had a different name for him then. Mwari according to the Shona people, uMlimu as the Ndebele people knew him. It is rumoured that Mwari's voice was last heard in 1974, the year I was born. Baba believes that I'm a quiet girl for that reason. I think deeply about a lot of things.

Maiguru says we've lost our ways. She says we've forgotten our songs and our dances because our tongues were cut off and replaced with English ones. It's the reason why we cannot pronounce our own names, why we no longer observe the sacred practice of rain making ceremonies. Here in the city, people do not believe in these pilgrimages to the hills. They do not believe in the art of dancing for rain. We clap like our former colonial masters, instead of *kuombera maoko* as the elders do. We do not know how to ululate like our grandmothers before us, a sweet, joyous and celebratory sound the tongue makes in the orchestra of its mouth. We were taught to wear shoes, so our feet forgot to communicate with the bareness of the soil. Maiguru always measures her words when she speaks.

"The settlers took our spiritual capital and built a church above the well from which our mediums used to drink. That's why we have these water problems."

There are many speculations about our past. Some think the hidden well in Matopos is a reservoir of infinite knowledge, a place where one could drink and find clarity, a source of healing for those afflicted with sickness, and an avenue to ask forgiveness for the wrong doings of mankind. Maybe it's the reason the English buried Cecil John Rhodes in the rocks of our kopje kingdom.

Maiguru is knitting on the rupasa and I reflect upon her sentiments as I cook. It's just the three of us now. My father, my mother's sister and I. We do not speak of the other family members we lost all those years ago. Sometimes, the leaves of Gogo's banana tree whistle in the wind, sometimes it sounds like laughter from a faraway time. I'm always listening for their voices the way I listen for water, but it does not come…

***

So, this is what the future looks like. 1995.

Humanity has made some progression. It has also committed the most atrocious crimes against itself.

Ha! And they thought they would have flying cars by now.

South Africa is fresh out of Apartheid, a year-old learning to walk on its newly found independent feet. Our darling Zimbabwe is a teenager. Fifteen and full of promise. Her president has been knighted by the Queen herself for being an anti-colonial hero. The world has lovingly nicknamed her the breadbasket of Africa, but they don't know that she only has five years' worth of crumbs left to give. We have been watching over our beloved for centuries if not millennia. We have witnessed her fight and struggle.

The cold dark nights of enslavement to the warm radiant days of sovereignty. Or so they thought.

We do not know how we came to be guardians of this place. We do not know much of our own beginning except that we began somewhere. I am a river flowing out of the timeless waters before me, Zambezi to Limpopo, forming tributaries of matriarchal blood. We keep returning to this place where the smoke is always rising. Bulawayo. The place of slaughter. This is where all the memories of the world were kept.

Before the invention of computers and databases, records, archives of golden information, were stored in the memories of mediums. They were the living libraries that walked amongst the people, and everyone knows that to destroy a book you must first break its spine, so their backbones were scarred with sjamboks, sliced open at the hands of the oppressor. Their heads were cut off and taken away as trophies of war. Colonialism.

The white settlers have gone. Even the one they call Livingstone who named our waters after his queen Victoria, he is no longer here.

We already had a name before his arrival. Mosi oa Tunya – *the smoke that thunders.*

It is long after Lozikeyi's time. Long after the reign and fall of Lobengula, son of Mzilikazi. From the 1800s to 1980.

We witnessed it all.

We were there when the liberation fighters consulted at Njelele in the second Chimurenga war. We were there when victory was established, and we witnessed a nation reborn. But we were soon forgotten when the fighting began again. This time amongst brothers born of the same blood. Sons of the soil. The greed has contaminated everything. They fight over the sacred places. They fight to own that which they did not create, to name it after themselves. How can one be custodian of where God resides? People sell water to each other from hosepipes, a dollar a bucket. Water? A resource that was freely created for all? Water is life, and no life comes with a price tag. But in this realm, they value profits over love and unity.

They no longer use smoke signals to communicate. They own telephones and fax machines. They wear denim jeans and drive automobiles. They worship the objects of their own creation, forgetting that they too are merely created things.

We thought after freedom had been granted, all would work together in harmony for the good of the people, but power corrupts absolutely. We witnessed the present leaders cut down their own people like trees.

It is a culture of repression slowly brewing, one that will bleed into decades of rule to come. A tradition of sacrifice for power.

They have chosen to make rain of their own. Blood rain. Gukurahundi. And they wonder why it does not rain anymore when the earth is swollen with the bodies of innocent victims that we carried away in our waters.

It is a pattern that we have had time to study over the centuries and mankind still fails the test.

These children of Nehanda do not understand.

They keep making the same mistakes in each decade, refusing to learn from the faults of their fathers. They do not know the ancient truths, and even those who do, do not treasure them. It is chaos woven into the fabric of ignorance. A generational occurrence of pain and suffering.

Their leaders trust in global health experts and put their faith in accumulating data and statistics, conducting extensive research. They see only what their science allows them to see, but they cannot test for the metaphysical aspect of geography. They cannot see what we have been given permission to see. Where science is not permitted to look. Where her boundaries end and ours begin.

And even in her world of mathematics and chemistry, we exist quietly, for it is us who carry the minerals and wealth of this nation.

Humans, even the so-called intellectuals or the most garnished and decorated of individuals, are simple creatures.

They test the mineral content of the soil, but they cannot see the marks of genocide scarring the land.

The earth remembers. She carries the dead in her body. She carries the living too, and in the agriculture of food, where crops grow out of dead father's corpses, a generation of sons and daughters are fed the fertile sorrows of many lives past without ever realising it.

Being daughters of the water, we take the shape of any human container. It is how we gather information for the current period in which mankind is living. I have worn this girl's body for almost twenty-two years now. We co-exist peacefully. Her thoughts are mine as mine are hers. She is a lover of rain, and her spirit has loved the sound of water since she was a little girl. I don't know why she was chosen for me, but I feel she has a good heart. Her memories of youth flood my periphery. She is thinking of a boy she loves, forgetting that her father is waiting expectantly for his midday meal.

Sweat pools under her arms and she thinks of the heat between her legs when Malachi kissed her last night. The texture of his lips, a delicious secret on hers. If all things have memory, she muses, does the rock we sat on still carry the warmth of our illicit affair?

Even the field in which she was conceived remembers the outline of her parents' silhouettes in the grass. Two figures intertwined in love. The ground where her mother's body would be found motionless, years later, dead at the hands of soldiers, remembers the stain of her blood and the colour of her dress.

It sounds like people are dancing in the sky. It sounds like the clapping of hands and the beating of drums. Mpilo secures her mother's head wrap and closes her eyes in sweet anticipation. A cool breeze blows across her face, lifting the knots of her thick, dark braids.

Is that…

No, it can't be. Could it be a miracle? Is that rain forming? The metallic scent of it, caresses her nose. Are those clouds gathering? She mutters a fervent prayer imploring the skies. Her lips move like bullets in a pistol, puncturing the air, and then it falls ever so lightly. The first drop. A second.

Drip, drip… those sparkling liquid gems of water she recalls from childhood.

"Mpilo, what are you doing?" Her aunt looks up in disbelief. "Are you… Are you…"

Her father whose posture is that of a withered tree begins to unfold like a flower. He is laughing a hearty chortle. A laugh that lights up the wrinkles on his face and illuminates his worn-out smile. Tears glisten in the eyes.

"She is calling the rain just like her mother… All along you had her gift."

Decades from now, when she is no longer a girl but an ageing woman, when her thick, oily braids are streaked with slivers of lightning grey, and the leaders of this time have finally relinquished power, she will be the one they call to bring back the rain.

Beverley Abrahams

Beverley Ann Abrahams is a teacher of English and Art (39 years), an activist against gender-based violence with DD4P, Daughters Destined For Purpose, a UK based charity in Zimbabwe (10 years) and a writer. She is mother to four children and a Christian.

Coloured Like Water
Beverley Abrahams – Zimbabwe

"No kaffirs in the store. Use the window."

Head gently lowered, finger pointing emphatically to the grey door. The words enunciated dispassionately, to a non-entity, one whose name meant nothing to him. She froze for just a second, then felt the blood pounding in her ears, like a pestle crushing maize at the end of the dry season, dissonant sounds as the kernels crushed and broke. They were the only customers in the store on that hot Friday afternoon, 2pm, middle of a summer's day bathed in brilliant blue skies. The dusty burglar-barred windows were in stark contrast to the papers plastered on the walls, advertising the weekly specials, bright like children's paintings. They had jumped out of the car minutes before, Elspeth chattering away like always, holding onto her arm. He was in his khaki work clothes, worn broad-brimmed hat over his blonde hair, wearing the spectacles that he could no longer avoid.

"*Uxolo*, sorry baas." She bowed her head in deference, playing a part that was unavoidable.

She had shrunk back at the familiar word 'kaffir', but it struck still like a shove in the chest that leaves you breathless. She walked quickly out the door, after pushing the child towards its father. He had not moved from the spot in front of the paint containers and shovels neatly aligned against the wall, jaw clenched tight, silent like water; he was seething but forced to be silent. She knew that if she hesitated, he might explode and do the unthinkable, defend a kaffir. He had called her into the store with the child, in the madness of reconciliation, not thinking; they had been laughing and singing in the car!

He clutched his child's hand tightly, as though he could somehow make up for this scene she would not have understood, so he thought. He sheltered her from the daily upheavals by keeping her home on the farm at Fort Rixon, within the fence and locked gate; the children did not mix with white families, and certainly not with the workers' children, theirs was a different reality. But he did not know the colours of his children's thoughts.

"Bloody Afrikaaners! Full of shit! Fuck them!"

He felt his betrayal of her keenly, the rules never changed, not even for a magistrate. He knew, too, of the talk that flowed from the loose-lipped community, the derision barely hidden behind social chit-chat and unlimited alcohol, whenever they met at the clubs or galas or barbecues. A 'kaffir-lover' they called him; he had fathered three children by the woman, and 'paraded his spawn like an insult' on his farm. The women were particularly venomous, despite their puritanical demeanour of Christianity. He despised the double standards that allowed them to treat black workers like slaves in their homes and on the streets, all in the face of their loving God who had sent them to rescue the natives from ignorance! He understood the sentiment, it was not foreign to him, but living amongst black people, so isolated and strange, what were you supposed to do? Despite his disdain of their criticism of him, he needed their acceptance into that small community. He knew he could not survive without their support, especially since his appointment by the mayor to the post of magistrate. A few tactful words had been said; they struggled to castigate their own; and how many had not stained their own hands? "We must do our part to uphold community standards, Callum, you know this fickle lot, they will destroy you on a whim if you give them half the chance. Best to keep a distance, hey, let them know who's baas". He hated that word! Most of the time, he pretended it did not matter, but this last year had brought him to breaking point!

He acknowledged his children, loved them, but keeping those worlds apart, ah, that was the hard part. There was no rule book that taught you how to love what society taught you to despise.

He turned back to the counter, placed his order in terse tones, teeth gritted in anger, counted the money onto the counter then marched out the door. She sat in the back seat, head against the windowpane, a dark statue, her stiff back and folded arms a curated rebellion. He jumped in, slid the child between the front seats to her. Her curly blond hair and stark blue eyes belied her heritage; her mother would always look like a servant. She enfolded the child into her arms without turning her head to face him.

"*Uxolo*," in a shamed voice.

"*Ngiyezwa*. I understand," in soft undertones.

She knew he was sorry. He was not a cruel man, and she was not just a servant. She would always be like the weeds in his garden, ever present but not what he cultivated. She often wondered these days, if he thought about the consequences of that fateful evening, years ago, amid the beauty of a dying sky, when he chose her.

Coloured children sprinkled the villages and farms like multi-coloured grains, yet that white community closed ranks against them all as though they were lepers. Bedding a black woman, impregnating her, that was nothing – the children were collected after a few years, placed in homes, given surnames like George, Charles and John, a curated collection of misfits taught to spit upon their black mother's shameless heads. But who knew what they carried in their hearts?

Callum was different, he never took another woman into his life, not until Miss Felicity. In four years, they had settled into a familiar routine, always with compromise, but bearable nevertheless. She stayed in the main house now, slept with the younger child; the older two had a separate bedroom. His door was three steps across from hers, it opened and closed silently. There was never noise, no words spoken, for they would only lie like a mountain on a road to a destiny that did not exist in the real world of Rhodesia. In living like he did, he knew he was breaking the law, one he was now appointed to uphold.

The shop assistant came out with his bags of supplies, nose flaring in contempt at seeing the little white girl curled up, asleep, on the servant's lap. Mr Murray jumped out of the car, opened the back of the station wagon and packed the supplies. He was a taciturn man at worst, but today he was just rude, throwing his money on the counter like they were beneath him. *Lucky Mr Potgeiter wasn't serving today. Did he think that being a magistrate gave him special powers? Why wasn't that woman in the back? The audacity of these Europeans with their uncivilised habits. Dirty, that's what they were! That poor child forced to sleep on the lap of a servant, had she bathed, how clean was she? Where on earth was the mother? Such shameless behaviour!*

Callum felt the slight in the eyes that evaded his, as though even that human contact would make him complicit in a crime. He felt his anger bubbling up but pushed it down. He could not afford another confrontation; it had cost too much already.

Four months ago, the Campbells unpacked into the farming community of Fort Rixon, newly arrived, nothing had prepared them for the heat and dust of September. Dust covered the shrubs, burnt blonde already by months of drought, and the grass was a mere shadow of a covering across the rolling vleis. The shimmering heat was blinding and made work in the sun near impossible. Unless hand-fed, the cattle rapidly lost weight, but the brahmin and *nguni* were tough, tougher than their masters! The middle-aged couple acquired the farm and its workers. The house was built of stone, cool in summer, cold in winter, comfortable for Europeans. They sent their teenage boy to the local mission school for white boys, determined to work to become another success in the cattle farming community that was thriving and well-respected in Bulawayo. Their daughter would follow in two months' time, once she had finished her college diploma as a teacher. Mr Campbell had been inducted into the local farmers group and advised to "not let the locals take advantage, they were a difficult lot, needed discipline to keep them in check." Within weeks, trouble erupted on the farm when Mr Campbell took a belt to a young man who had not reported for duty on time. Overnight, six of his workers disappeared and could not be found in the village. He turned to his neighbour, Callum Murray for help, and he willingly obliged. In twenty-four hours, the workers reappeared, were docked three days' pay as a deterrent, and peace was restored.

The Campbells had not heard the gossip about Callum, and besides, he was a kinsman. A few days later, he was invited for sundowners at their farm; and thus began the habit of spending two to three evenings a week at the Campbells'. He realised how much he missed the camaraderie of kindred spirits, those who could share in his reminiscence of home. Home was becoming an improbable dream against this African landscape that stretched you to breaking point. Many broke: malaria, alcohol and loneliness. Sindisiwe stayed home with the children, often keeping them awake as long as possible so they could see him before they slept. He'd often return late, sometimes drunk, but more often, just happy, a happiness that she could not understand, it was not the happiness of home. Suspicions rose like bitter bile, but she knew she was bound to a silence and compliance that could not be broken with words. Too often, his door of invitation did not open, and she never presumed. Servitude was like a rock around her neck, she never forgot her place.

Two months later, the pattern changed. He took more care with his appearance, he bought new clothes, shaved cleanly, insisted the gardener wash the car before he left. She would never forget the day he threw his white shirt back in her face, swearing loudly that she was lazy and not doing her job. "*Suka, hamba*! Go, get out!" Careless words intoned like poison. In that moment of stunned silence, something broke in the still December air, with its seamless blue skies that blended into the haze of the land, a crack like thunder that would change forever the narrow world in which she'd believed she was safe. She did not raise her eyes from his newly polished shoes that shone with her labour, did not move a muscle. She was reminded of that great divide that separated them from a conversation about right and wrong. She ironed another shirt, laid it carefully over the back of the spotless dining chair, while he lay slumped in an armchair in stony silence. She curtseyed to him, eyes fixed to the floor and walked slowly out the back door into the vegetable garden, followed the footpath through its multitude of sprouting beds filled with onions, tomatoes, peas, carrots and the radishes that he loved, and crossed over the fence into the small copse of *musasa* trees that were resplendent in their summer green leaves. Here, in that solitary space, she finally cried, silent tears of regret. She flung herself at the foot of the *hute* tree, ignoring the fallen purple fruit that would stain her dress like menstrual blood.

"Useless tears, I'm just a whore! *Ngiyisifebe nje*! What did I expect from a white man who does not belong to me?"

He returned home later that night. She always left a paraffin lantern on the kitchen counter so he could find his way. She wouldn't sleep until she knew he was home safe. As he walked down the stone paved path to the house, he heard the faint sounds of cicadas singing in the singed grass beyond the fence. It had not rained for countless days, and the heat was oppressive, like a plastic bag over his head. Tonight, their sound reminded him of mourning, that high keening sound of an African woman's sorrow. He had enjoyed the night, it had been a success. Felicity had welcomed him so warmly, the touch of her hand in his fingers still lingered like her magnolia perfume! So why did he feel so deflated entering his own home? He dropped his clothes by the side of his bed, climbed in quietly, wary of the creak of the sprung bed. He wanted to be left alone with his thoughts tonight. Besides, she was probably tired out by now, he had left her alone all day and night with three energetic children, but she was strong; there was little she couldn't do without him.

Morning broke with the sounds of birds which had become like an alarm to his day – warblers, starlings and turacos in rising and falling crescendos. The sharp trill of a Cape robin sounded just outside his open window, mingling with the sounds of voices drifting across the fields. He imagined their words floating like smoke into the freshness of the morning. He dressed quickly – she made sure his clothes were put out at night for the next morning – then went into the kitchen. The table was carefully laid, a spotless white tea towel covered the breakfast tray. Normally, she was at the wood range, waiting to serve him, humming a tune. The porridge was simmering on the corner of the wood range, far enough to not burn. His tea flask was filled. There was not a sound. He checked the two bedrooms, they were empty, beds neatly made. She must have taken the children for a walk. He ate in silence, left the house unlocked and drove into town.

She watched him drive away, then returned to the house after the dust from his car had settled like ash from a fire. The day dragged painfully slow. She cleaned and cooked, and by 5pm had bathed the children. At 5.30pm, she fed them and settled them into their rooms, whispering her love into their ears like cool raindrops, "*Ngiyakuthanda, lisale kuhle,*" and bidding them goodnight. She laid the kitchen table for him, they usually ate together. At 6.00pm, fifteen minutes before he was due home, she was on the path that crossed the small stream, on her way to the village, a cloth bag of her belongings slung across her back, a basket with a few vegetables from the garden balanced on her head. She walked into the sunset, a grey shadow coalescing into darkness by the time his car parked under the huge *mhunondo* tree where the owls slept.

He opened the door reluctantly. She was probably still angry, she had become more short-tempered of late; he hoped she wasn't pregnant again! The house was too quiet. Again, the table was neatly laid but with only one plate, his dinner on the corner of the stove, at a slow simmer. His heart slowed in fear, anxiety like a chokehold. He heard the tinkle of voices and found the three children in the one bedroom, the two younger ones already asleep. Elspeth was playing with the blue-eyed doll he'd bought for her fourth birthday. It was wrapped in colourful rags, cut offs from Sindisiwe's old dress.

"Where's mama?"

"She said good night and went?"

"Went? Went where, Elspeth?"

"I don't know. She took her dress and her basket daddy. She was crying daddy."

His heart sank. So it had come to this cat-and-mouse game again! It took a few drinks of whiskey for the fire of anger to rise, but he could not go shouting her name into the darkness that blanketed the surroundings like a cloak of invisibility. He would not go to her father's house to collect her! He knew her family despised him. He still thought he'd saved her.

He would deal with her in the morning.

"Bloody woman, what was her problem! Let her stay in the dirt of her father's hut tonight, she will be back tomorrow!"

A restless night and a hangover did not bode well for the sunrise that was as inevitable as the confrontation to come. He heard the muted knock on the door while the house was still misted in the grey of darkness. He had been up for hours already. She wore a white doek over her braided hair and did not look at his face.

"Morning baas."

The words stung him, and he had to restrain himself from slapping her across the face.

"Why did you go? You left the children alone!"

"They have their father baas. I went home, baas."

The silence deepened. There were no words to speak of what had to remain unsaid.

Seven days passed in thunderous silence, heavy with the weight of regret and love, coiled like snakes. Each evening, she put the children to bed, set his dinner table and went to the village across the river. On the following Thursday, as she was walking through the door, he informed her that he would have a visitor on the Friday evening. She was to prepare the meal and take the children to sleep in the servant quarters behind the house. He did not want to be disturbed.

"*Uyaqonda*?" Do you understand?

"*Ngikuqonde khale* baas." I understand perfectly.

The battle lines were drawn. Her servility irritated him like an acacia thorn in the heel because he knew it hid an iron core that he could not penetrate; he wanted to shake her, hit her, he wanted something from her that he could not explain. He stormed out of the house, the windows reverberating from the slam of the door.

The sunset painted the sky in orange, red and pink. It looked like a pale blue scarf dipped in blood. The raucous crows floated high in the sky, turning in a gyre like blackened embers caught in a whirlwind. He parked the car under the tree and quickly walked around to the passenger door to open it. Felicity stepped out; she had dressed up for the evening with him. She wore a starched, long yellow dress, far too hot for the summer heat. Her mother had chosen it, she believed Callum was conservative, did not want a 'forward' wife. She was pretty, slender, pale, ethereal and fragile. He felt as if she would break like a clay pot if she fell onto the bricked walkway. They strolled around the yard first, she dutifully admired the neat, solid home surrounded by a trellised veranda, dotted with plants in plastic buckets. The straggly fruit trees cast long, thin shadows and looked like accusatory ghosts in that dimming summer dusk. She shrunk back at the owl that flitted sharply out of a huge tree that umbrellaed the corner of the yard where he parked the car.

Already, she was beginning to regret having come out to this country, couldn't understand how her parents were enjoying it. Of course, they were the privileged class here, but the debilitating heat and dust was unbearable. Everyone drank far too much, and even the women smoked! She hoped to meet a good man and settle down, perhaps join one of the mission schools. Her mother had encouraged her to leave her grandparents and join them as there were many men out here looking for good wives. She liked Callum as soon as she met him, he was soft-spoken, shy, with those striking blue eyes and white-blond hair, he stood out in the crowd. When she first saw him, as he strolled up the driveway to their house, he looked like a golden god, shimmering in sunset. After four weeks of visiting her at her home, he had finally invited her for a meal at his.

Sindisiwe watched them through the window, heart-stopped, feeling like she could not breathe. She had hoped it was not a woman, but gossip had already started about his visits to the Campbells'. He had been seen at the country club in her company. There were many of her people happy to throw his behaviour in her face! *"Manje uphi umuntu wahko*?" And now, where is your man? Perhaps she had grown proud at being his chosen one?

Callum opened the front door, expecting it to be empty. He smelt lavender even before he saw her standing by the stove, back turned to the door. For a moment, his heart sank in fear, but he would not show it. When she turned, she saw the stony look of anger on his face.

"*Salibonani* baas, *salibonani* madam," and she curtseyed. "The food is ready."

He could not answer, but blushed red in his confusion. Felicity had already walked ahead of him into the sitting room area, ignoring the servant. She still had difficulty understanding their guttural accents. Sindisiwe's head was uncovered, neatly braided, a wild, white oleander blossom tucked behind her ear. He did not recognise the long, African print dress that she was wearing.

She carried the covered dishes of food to the table then stood aside as though to serve him. He flicked his fingers in dismissal, but she did not move, eyes fixed on the floor. He called Felicity to the table, carefully drew out the chair for her to sit on. He asked Felicity to serve while he turned to pour their drinks, hands shaking with the turmoil of emotions that he could not suppress. She touched his hand as she passed the plate to him. Sindisiwe watched in contempt and pain. She had not felt pain like this since giving birth to their last child who was breach and almost killed her. Something inside her felt like a monster tearing through her bones with a knife. She walked quickly out the front door and closed it behind her before slipping down onto the concrete stoep. The cold against her palms slowly reminded her of her place, of who she was. She tossed the white flower into the thickening darkness.

She would not leave, and an hour later, she re-entered the house. They were sitting in armchairs, facing each other, talking in low, intimate tones. He froze. She cleared the table, taking her time by carrying just a few items at a time to the steel sink. Callum stopped talking. From the kitchen, she overheard Felicity ask him, "Is your servant wearing lavender perfume? I can smell her!"

He felt so ashamed. "It's just soap, leftovers that she must have taken. You know these servants, always pinching stuff."

She smiled to herself, imagining how furious he must be. He had given her a bar of lavender soap when she had started bathing in the house, and she kept it for special nights.

She finished in the kitchen, leaving everything spotlessly clean, his breakfast tray covered on the counter, and walked silently out the door. She knew she had ruined his evening. By the time she disrobed and jumped into bed with the children, she heard the sound of his car starting up. He was taking Felicity home already. She felt happier than she had been for weeks.

Something shook her awake! Her mind was rattled for a few seconds until she recognised what it was. His footsteps on the gravel must have woken her. She felt his presence against the door even though there was no sound now. There was the lightest knock. She was spellbound, she was afraid to breathe in case he heard her. The feather-light tap against the door, a moan, suppressed rage. She would not answer tonight, not tonight.

She did not sleep. Every sound brought fear, yet she knew he would never intentionally harm her, would not disturb their children. She wanted him to suffer like she suffered, to feel what she'd been feeling for too long.

Morning brought the chaos of the children awakening and wanting to rush to see their father. She let them run to him, barefoot and in pyjamas, curly blonde hair in disarray. She heard the familiar shouts and peals of laughter as he embraced them, swinging them in the air. She slowly made up the narrow beds. It was a stark room, asbestos roof with no ceiling, blue painted walls, a small wooden shelf to hold a candle, a single window like a slash in a box. She had to face his anger, get over the night, and fight the giant standing between them.

She walked in on them with a wan smile and greeted him.

"*Livukile* baas." Good morning. There was no response other than the fury written on his pallid face. He would not raise his voice at her in front of the children. They loved her as much as they loved him. While he fumed at the table, she busied herself in the kitchen, singing to herself, knowing he could hear her.

"*Mangikhule lapho engitshalwe khona, ngiyeke ngibe ngumuntu engizalwa nginguye.*" Let me grow where I am planted, let me be who I was born to be.

"Let him believe that I don't care! It serves him right. *Anginandaba*! I don't care!"

The slump of his shoulders showed the burden of his torment, and she felt a pang of guilt. But he had made the choice, one she never had.

She served him and the children, as she always did, a role she had become accustomed to. She did not touch him, as she often did, glancing touches that lingered through her working day until the night which saw no colour. But what did he see when he saw her? Was he now comparing her to a white woman, is that what he now craved? Had he taken her from her father's house only to shame her by abandoning her with three mixed race children? They would never let her keep those children, if he left her! For the first time, she felt an overwhelming panic, and could not help the moan which escaped her lips – not her children! Not her children, never!

He hurried in, thinking she had cut herself. She was crouched over the sink, head bowed down.

"*Ulimele?*" Are you okay?

"*Ngizwa ubuhlungu.*" I'm in pain, she whispered back.

"*Lala, uphumule, ngiyacela.*" Lie down, rest, please. He spoke with concern, all anger gone.

She staggered to the bedroom, lay down as though her bones had melted and could not keep her soul together. She did not dare cry, for fear she would not be able to stop. He brought her tea, did not know what to say, could not stand the silence. Soon after, she heard the door bang and knew he had gone. Time did not give her answers, and she did not have the luxury of tears, the children were her responsibility and demanded attention. The day unwound, like all days did. By sunset, she was in the room at the back of the house, and the children were in their room in the house. She ached all over like a witch had beaten her! Maybe this is how death would take her…

This time, he knocked loudly, insistently, and when she did not answer, told her he would break the door down. He was not a man who wasted words. She opened the door quickly, she was still in her apron, doek sitting crookedly on her head. She knew that the gardener and the guard could hear his voice, but he seemed not to care, not tonight. He was sober, angry, and frustrated. He grabbed her hands and pulled her roughly outside, then lifted her into his arms and carried her into the house, back to her room, her bed. He lay her down, then walked out without a word. She lay as he had put her down, dress crumbled up above her knees, arms spread wide, heart pounding like a drum. She overheard him telling the children that she was sick and needed to rest.

"Why is mama sick, who made her sick?"

"I don't know my boy, she's just sick."

"I can look after her, I can make tea now daddy." This from Elspeth, always her protector.

"She will be better tomorrow, you be quiet, go to sleep. Say your prayers Elly," he said.

He put them to bed, planting a soft kiss on each brow. They were like puppies, demanding little, so grateful for the time he found to love them. Then she heard his slow footsteps, heard him close his door, as soft as a whisper.

He lay in his bed, fully clothed, exhausted and confused. What life was this that he had chosen? The blurred lines, the hard boundaries, they demanded a strength that he did not have. What a vain hope it had been that a woman like Felicity might want to be part of his life! He didn't love her of course, but she would be so acceptable, so easy to have, to hold, to see! What was love anyways, in this harsh world where hate bloomed like weeds and consumed like fire? She would never accept his children, no white woman would, but he could not leave them, and he did not know if he could leave Sindisiwe either.

The door creaked open slowly, and she stepped in. She hesitated for just a moment, until he turned his head towards her and saw her outlined in moonlight against the wall like a palpitating moth, her flimsy nightdress slipping off her shoulders, her hair a shiny halo, then she climbed into his bed. She did not touch him and turned her back as she lay balanced on the far edge of the bed. He reached towards her with trembling hands, pulling her close so she enveloped him in the heady smell of lavender, and held on to her like she was all he needed to save himself from the storms that lay ahead.

Elton Ndudzo

Elton Ndudzo is a twenty year old writer based in Chitungwiza, Zimbabwe. He writes fiction and explores themes of feminism, culture, and spirituality. He recently self-published his debut book, HWATA AND THE MANELESS WHITE on Amazon Kindle. He is also a student at Chinhoyi University, pursuing a degree in Computer Engineering. You can find him on X (formerly Twitter) @elton_writer and Instagram @eltonndudzo

In The Fold
Elton Ndudzo – Zimbabwe

Ruramo rolled his eyes as he saw the familiar sign that read, *Welcome to Great Zimbabwe.*

He just hated family vacations, especially to places that he had been to countless times. He dragged his feet behind his sister, mom and other tourists who were chatting excitedly with the tour guide. To make things worse, there was no network reception. He felt the sweat dripping from his forehead and the dust sticking to his skin. He wished he could escape the scorching heat and the boring history lesson. He already missed his cosy room, his comfy bed, and the PS5 Valentine gift.

"Whatever you do, do not touch anything without being told," the guide repeated. "And most importantly, DO NOT insult anything at all, not even a rock. You never know what might be listening."

Ruramo put on his headphones and turned up the volume, drowning out the guide's voice. He didn't care about the old stories and childish fables about the haunted ruins and disappearing men. He followed along as they walked down the narrow path leading to the old city. He felt bored and restless, wishing he was somewhere else. He wished that he could just disappear into those old, abandoned walls and never be found.

Somewhere along the path, Ruramo decided to stray away from the group to search for better network reception. He walked away from the main trail, hoping to find a clearing or a small hill where he could get a signal. He held up his phone, checking the bars, but they remained empty. He cursed under his breath, feeling frustrated and annoyed.

He then noticed a baboon staring at him. He tried to ignore it, but it did not move its eyes from him.

"What are you looking at, you ugly weirdo?" Ruramo shouted at the baboon, hoping to scare it away.

The baboon did not move or make a sound. It just tilted its head slightly and continued to stare at him. He felt like it was mocking him, amused at his misery. He wished he could punch it in the face, but he knew it was too far and too fast. He looked around for something to throw at it. He spotted a stone on the ground and picked it up. He aimed at the baboon's head and threw it with all his strength. He heard a satisfying thud and a loud screech. He grinned, feeling a surge of triumph.

He turned to look at his phone again, hoping to see some bars or a message. But the screen was blank and dark. He pressed the power button. Nothing happened. He figured the battery was dead. A curse ripped from his lips, sharp and bitter.

He lurched to his feet in frustration, then looked around to realise that he couldn't see anyone or anything familiar in sight. Confusion gnarled at him as he spun around, realising that he was alone and deep in the wild. He didn't remember wandering quite far from the monument. The ground beneath his feet was now slick with damp leaves, and he was very sure that it was all dry just moments ago.

"Hello? Chido, mom? Is anyone there?" Ruramo called out, his voice shaking with fear. He pushed through the tangled forest, hoping to find his way back to the group.

"Yes, there is someone here," a rich and deep voice emerged from behind him. Ruramo spun around, his scream piercing the air as he beheld a tree. It was no ordinary tree, but one with breasts, and a mouth that spoke and eyes that saw.

Ruramo rubbed his eyes and shook his head, trying to dispel the surreal scene from his mind. It couldn't possibly be real.

"You stand within the fold, young boy," the tree spoke to him in a voice that sounded ancient and wise. "It is the veil between your world and the ancestral one."

"No, this isn't real, you shouldn't be real," Ruramo said, as he shook his head. "It's impossible. You are a tree, you cannot talk, you shouldn't be…"

"Perhaps in your world, but not the fold," the tree told him. "We once existed within your world a long time ago, *pasichigare*. Have you so quickly forgotten what you are told in your stories, of when rivers climbed up mountains, stones had ears, and donkeys had horns? All that is now gone from your world but exists in the fold."

"Yes, it does indeed," Ruramo heard a high-pitched voice next to him. He turned down to see that it was a stone, with a mouth and eyes and ears. He gasped and covered his mouth with his hand. "You thought it was only you humans, who only could see and speak, didn't you?"

"I'm not supposed to be seeing all of this, I'm not supposed to be here," Ruramo muttered. "Why am I in the fold at all? How did I even get here?"

"You are here because you insulted something that you should've not, young boy," the tree told him. "Everything around the ancient palace is important and should be respected, and those that fail to do that are trapped in the fold."

Ruramo then remembered the incident earlier, with the baboon. "Excuse me! I'm innocent in this. The baboon was the one staring at me in the first place. I was just minding my own business."

"Well, the baboon clearly didn't see it that way," the tree said. "The mukanyas quite have a temper. You are already getting late. If the sun sets before you find the baboon and seek his forgiveness, you shall live in this fold forever and ever. Now, journey west, and seek this creature you offended before it's too late."

Ruramo had not wanted to do this but found that he had no other choice. He was very frustrated but then just decided to go and ask for forgiveness and get it over with.

"I don't know which way west is by the way," he said, a frown on him.

"Humans never really change, do they," the tree said, then went on to point west for him with one of its branches.

"Good luck young boy," the stone with ears told the boy before he departed. "Stay out of danger, monsters also lurk within the fold."

A cold shiver moved through his body when he heard about monsters. He had never believed in monsters, but after what he had seen, he knew better.

Ruramo nodded his head at the stone, then departed to seek this baboon that he had so offended.

Everything going on was just crazy and unbelievable. He would soon awaken from his dream, he thought to himself. He wasn't seriously on his way to go and ask for forgiveness from a baboon.

Ruramo thought he was going to walk a long way, but before long, he had reached the territory of the baboons. He did not realise that he was already in their territory until the moment he turned to look up.

He beheld hundreds of baboons sitting on the branches above him, looking down at him with their judging eyes. He looked ahead, and his eyes landed on *the* baboon, sitting in his path. He could see that his arrival had been greatly anticipated.

"Shame," one of the baboons sitting on the branches above him shouted. "He should not be forgiven!"

Ruramo wanted to scream with anger but managed to keep himself cool and calm. What he needed was to get his forgiveness and get himself out of this strange place.

"I'm surely in a dream," he whispered to himself as he stood right in front of the baboon. He had to hold himself from screaming with anger when he delivered his apologies. "Mr baboon, I'm sorry if you were offended by my acts earlier. Can you please forgive me, because I've got to get going. My fam must be worried sick, not knowing where I am."

"Louder, we can't hear a thing back here," another baboon from the trees protested. Ruramo wished there was a stone nearby so that he could hit this annoying baboon with it.

He then cleared his throat again, and repeated his apology, now louder.

"That's no proper way to apologise, you ought to address him as the great Mukanya that he is," one baboon protested. "You said that he was ugly, that is the greatest insult one can ever make."

A murmur of agreement rose from the rest of the baboons.

"He should also be on his knees and clapping his hands," another one added. "He is so disrespectful, no wonder he is trapped in the fold."

Ruramo looked back with a frown, wanting to find the baboon that had spoken, but he just saw hundreds of baboons in the trees looking back at him. They were all waiting for him to apologise properly.

Ruramo looked back at the baboon as it was just sitting there, waiting for a proper apology. Ruramo couldn't imagine himself, with his own pride, on his damn knees, asking for an apology from the baboon, in front of hundred other baboons. It was not even an insult, but plain truth. They were *all* a bunch of ugly weirdos.

No human was watching, just these baboons that would remain in the fold. If he got on his knees, no one would ever know, he told himself.

So, Ruramo set aside all his pride, went on his knees, and started clapping with cupped hands at the baboon. "Great one, oh great Mukanya. Please forgive me for throwing a stone at you and calling you an ugly weirdo. I didn't mean it at all. Your handsomeness is a wonder to behold. The girls would scream if they ever came across you. I hope you find a place in your heart for forgiveness. Now I've got to get going soon, before it gets too late."

"You are mocking him, aren't you?" a second baboon dropped from the branch of a tree with a thud and walked right to him. This one was larger and more menacing than the one he had offended. His eyes bore into Ruramo's with a cold fury. "Are you really serious about leaving this fold? Do you think that this is a game, that we have all gathered here to watch you make fun of us?"

The baboon wanted to scare him, wanted to act like he was the big boss. Ruramo had not insulted *him*, and he should just stay out of a matter that didn't concern him.

"No, I don't think that this is a game," Ruramo managed to say, rising to his feet. "I think this is a dream, and soon I'll get to wake up from it."

He barely saw the paw that struck his face. A sharp pain exploded in his cheek, and he stumbled backwards, falling to the ground. He blinked, trying to clear his vision. He tasted blood in his mouth. He heard a roar of anger above him. "Now, do you still think you are in a dream?" the baboon bellowed. Ruramo looked up and saw him looming over him, his teeth bared. "Have you awakened from it? This isn't like those stupid tales that you tell one another, idiot. Now, get back on your knees, and beg my son for an apology, sincerely."

Ruramo felt a tear roll down his face. He had not known that this was the father to *the* baboon. He wanted to run, to hide, to escape. But he knew he had no choice. He had to face the consequences of his actions. He glanced at the other baboon, the one he had insulted.

He saw a flicker of compassion in his eyes. "Please father," the baboon said softly. "It's ok, he has already asked for forgiveness."

"Shall I say it again?" the father-baboon asked, his eyes still glaring at Ruramo. "On your knees!"

Ruramo turned to look up at the other baboons sitting on the tree branches, their faces etched with cold, unforgiving disdain. Tears, hot and humiliating, streamed down his cheeks, mixing with the snot dribbling from his nose. Never had he felt so utterly, soul-crushingly small.

A strangled sob escaped his lips as he crumpled to his knees, hands clasped in a desperate plea before the baboon he had offended. "Please," he begged, his voice hoarse and broken, "forgive me. I made a mistake. I'll never do it again, I promise, please, please have mercy!"

The baboon inclined its head, a curt, dismissive gesture, accepting the apology. Then, the world dissolved into darkness.

After a beat, he awoke to the frantic calls of his sister, her voice cutting through the darkness. He opened his eyes and saw her worried face, wet with tears, hovering over him. "What happened?" he asked, dazed and confused.

"You had a seizure," she said softly, hugging him tightly. "But it's over now, you're safe. You're okay, don't be scared."

"You've no idea what I've been through," he said, and then he couldn't hold it in any longer. He buried his face in her shoulder, crying his heart out. His sister held him close, her whispers a balm against the searing wounds of humiliation that he had endured.

Tafadzwa Madzika

Tafadzwa Madzika is a nomad of the digital world, a storyteller and curator of the arts. He is a writer, content creator, poet, arts and entertainment reporter, mental health and disability rights advocate. He has contributed to platforms such as Greedysouth, Enthuse Magazine and Foodies 263. He expresses himself creatively in multiple mediums of art because he believes our ideas should be lived out instead of boxed in within our comfort zones. He is passionate about lending a hand to the community and uplifting others, which has seen him work as Mandisa Trust's goodwill ambassador and become one of the founding trustees of Kuyamura Children's Trust.

The Politics Of Murder
Tafadzwa Madzika – Zimbabwe

If one had looked beside the bridge along Chiremba Road, where it traverses the Mukuvisi River, they would've noticed a black sedan stop and toss the body of a middle-aged man, swollen beyond recognition, with a severely bleeding headwound and an address written on his inner forearm. A guard's uniform was still recognisable on him. But it was the witching hour and pitch dark. People often got mugged and raped in that area at that time, so no one walked unless they were those doing the mugging and the raping, and no cars stopped.

If one had followed that black sedan, they would've seen it head into the Eastlea neighbourhood and drop off a young university student at a gate without a number, on a street that looked like any other. If one had been on that street, they would've seen the young lady was dressed in an oversized hoodie and slippers with nothing else on. She was visibly shaking as the car sped off and that wouldn't have been unusual, but it was the October heat wave in Harare and you could sleep naked outside.

If one had ignored the girl getting dropped off and carried on following the car, they would've seen it drive into the heart of the CBD and stop outside the central police station. They would've seen a constable approach the car and receive a package wrapped in a dirty cloth. The constable would unwrap the package, revealing a standard 9 mm pistol, and if one had been close enough, they would've noted the scent of gunpowder in the air. But no one noticed another dark sedan on another warm summer night in Harare, and so the nature of things took their own twisted course.

At precisely 4:03am of the Sunday morning, it started to drizzle just as the sun was beginning to chase the night away. Panga was just beginning his daily marathon of wandering. It's not that he still knew his name was Panga, but that's the name his parents had given him decades before. It had been a long time since he had known a home that wasn't the streets. Mental illness had withered away almost all his self-awareness, but still, bouts of lucidity and reasoning presented themselves.

As Panga delved to the sides of the bridge to start his daily collection of plastic bottles and the rain showers began, he was accosted by pained groaning. It froze him in place until he identified where it was coming from. On seeing the barely moving body, he started to scream. It was incoherent but loud. He ran back up to the road and kept shouting while pointing down to where the body was. The first car passing by stopped for him, packed with several teenagers returning from a night of drinking.

It didn't take long before the barely breathing man was carried up to the road and an ambulance was on the way. No wallet, ID or phone were found on him, but that wasn't unusual for a victim of mugging in the area. However, everyone was drawn to his right inner forearm. Written with an indelible marker was, *1708 Bounty Crescent, Budiriro*, an address where a loving wife was waiting for her husband to arrive any hour now.

***

Across the city, in the affluent northern suburbs, there was commotion of nearly the same sort. Several police cars were parked outside the minister's house. The minister sat on the front steps with dried blood caked on his hands, visibly distraught. The lounge of his house showed clear evidence of a struggle, and lying motionless on the kitchen floor, with several bullet wounds, was the minister's wife. Blood had pooled all around her and it was long dry. Her corpse was long cold. She had her eyes wide open in permanent shock and horror.

"So what time was it again you heard the sound downstairs?" asked a detective standing next to the minister.

"Around one thereabouts, I didn't check the exact time."

"Tell me what happened when you came downstairs."

"There were two guys in the lounge… Well, I only saw two guys fleeing when I finally came down. My wife came down first, she thought it was our daughter and the next thing I heard were gunshots."

"How long was it between her coming down and…"

"Enough questions! Leave the minister alone now," barked a bulky man in a dark suit who had just arrived on the scene. Nothing identified who he was, but everyone immediately deferred authority to him. The questioning of the minister was over and there was no argument about it. It's just how things worked in Harare. You knew your place and when to speak because a lot of the times your life would depend on it. It didn't take long before the minister was cleared out of there and driven to a hotel on the outskirts of town.

***

To the east of the city, in the neighbourhood of Eastlea, a young woman woke up with a striking headache and a mouth bone dry from thirst. She had passed out on top of the blankets without bothering to change or having the presence of mind to do so. Answering nature's call, she got up and headed to the bathroom. Afterwards, she headed out to the kitchen for some water.

"Michelle you're here!" exclaimed Vimbai as the young woman entered the kitchen.

"Yeah, I got in late last night," she replied.

"I thought you were sleeping over at your parents' house."

"Plans changed babe, you know."

Michelle had arrived at the shared rental house in the early hours of the morning. They were two other girls she lived with, and they were in their second year at the University of Zimbabwe. Early in their first-year studies, while living on campus, they had struck up a friendship and eventually convinced each other to move off campus. The mobility offered by Michelle's car had been the biggest convincing factor, a red Mercedes Benz C200 that was less than five years old.

But in the background of all these factors, Michelle had been long awaiting the chance to get away from her parents, her mother mainly. Being the daughter of a career politician and trophy wife-slash-homemaker had its downsides. Her father belonged to politics more than he did to the family, and her mother poured everything she had into her. Right up to the point of trying to steer her every decision. So she had to escape. The new living arrangement gave her the freedom of mobility without needing permission and some privacy, but she was still economically dependent on her parents.

***

The injured John Doe arrived at Parirenyatwa Hospital conscious but still very much disoriented. A psychological evaluation was immediately ordered after he was admitted. It was the middle of a strike by nurses and doctors due to the underfunding of government hospitals, so only the casualty ward was operational, and to everyone else, they simply said may the best immune system win. After a visual scan of his injuries, the John Doe was put on a drip and ordered to take in as many fluids as possible. A nurse was going to find a way to him when gauzes for dressing his head wound were located.

The psychologist walked into his room and grabbed the clipboard at the end of his bed. There was no name on the chart, just an address and the observed injuries.

"Good morning, sir," said the psychologist.

"Good morning," the John Doe weakly replied.

"I'm Dr Nhema, what's your name?"

"I've been trying to figure that out since I got up, but I can't remember."

"So, what do you remember?"

There was nothing remotely linked to his identity that he could call up, but basic technical questions, he could answer. He was diagnosed with retrograde amnesia due to a severe concussion. There wasn't an estimate of when his memory would come back because no scans of him had been taken due to the striking workforce. So they simply hoped for the best and carried on.

The resident police officer at the hospital was summoned to the John Doe's room and told about how he was found and the address written on his inner right forearm. It had been an overall slow week for him, so he had time to look into the case. The address copied down, he was headed to Budiriro.

As Michelle finished eating at her shared house in Eastlea, her phone rang. It was a hidden number, but that didn't surprise her. She knew who often called with such security measures.

"Hello."

"Hey sweetie, there's a car coming to pick you up, please get ready."

"Okay daddy, let me get changed."

"Alright, see you soon."

"Bye."

If you had been on this street the previous night and you were paying attention, you would've noticed a black sedan, the same black sedan that would come today and pick up the same young woman it had dropped off the previous night. They would be no way of telling if the driver was still the same but what are the chances. If you had been near the bridge along Chiremba road last night and just so happened to be at Rainbow Towers hotel today, you would've seen the same black sedan that dumped the unconscious body of a man drive in and stop right in front of minister Moyo.

Michelle was greeted by her father as she exited the car at the hotel. They embraced and Michelle was instantly in tears.

"I'm sorry dad."

"It's okay my love, it's okay."

***

As Mrs Sevenzo was calling her husband for the 15th time, a police car arrived at her gate. She waved the police officer in while remaining seated at the veranda.

"Good afternoon mama," said the officer.

"Good afternoon officer, how can I help you?" she replied.

"I was wondering if you could identify someone," the officer said, passing Mrs Sevenzo his phone with the screen showing a picture of the John Doe at the hospital.

"Stephen! Oh my God!"

"So, you know him?"

"What happened to him?"

"He's in hospital. He was found beaten up and dumped in the morning."

After thirty minutes of conversation, a visibly worried Mrs Sevenzo locked up the house and left with the officer, headed to the hospital. She kept sending up silent prayers for her husband right up until they arrived. As she went into his room, the officer was calling headquarters that the John Doe was none other than Stephen Sevenzo, a security guard at Minister Moyo's house. And everyone had heard the news of the murder of the minister's wife.

An hour after the call, a bulky man in a dark suit walked into the army commander's office at the Freedom barracks. The policeman was already seated, the army commander opposite him, both in their full colours. The bulky man quietly took a seat next to the police commissioner and gently cleared his throat.

"Go ahead, report."

"Well as it stands, the police are working under the assumption that there was a break in and the burglars shot the minister's wife."

"Mmm…"

"But I've collected footage from our counter surveillance of senior government personnel after a rather unfortunate encounter with the minister's guard, and it shows an argument between the daughter and the minister's wife which ended with her shooting her mother."

"Do you know why?"

"We can't ascertain it, but Michelle's boyfriend was sleeping with the mother too."

"Interesting, very interesting. And the guard?"

"A result of the minister fumbling in his own attempt at a cover up."

"Ah, politics is his gift and not tactics."

"What's the way forward?"

"Add the footage and evidence to the operational folder, then notify the good minister of the price of this coverup!"

"Yes, sir."

***

If you were at the Rainbow Towers hotel that night, you would've noticed a black sedan drive into the car park. You would've seen a figure in a dark suit enter the hotel and head straight for the stairs. If you were on the fourth floor of the hotel, you would've seen the dark figure knock on room 458 before the minister opened it and he entered. The conversation did not last long behind the closed doors, and ten minutes later, the dark figure was on the go, leaving by the exact same route that he had got there.

If you were in the Parirenyatwa Hospital area that same night, you would've noticed the same black sedan drive in and head to the casualty ward. You would've seen several brown paper bags handed over to the doctor on duty that night, each one containing $2,500 in crisp hundred dollar bills. If you were close enough, you would've heard the man in the black sedan say, "As soon as he mentions anything to do with the minister, secure him in the psych ward and call us."

If you had read the papers in the days that followed, you would've seen the story of the minister's wife being allegedly murdered by burglars on the front page. A small section on the eigth page in the more liberal papers would mention a man found on the side of a bridge but nothing more. A few months later, Mr Sevenzo would end up dying of a supposed heart attack, and his wife would receive a very healthy severance cheque from the minister. Michelle would defer the first semester of her third year due to a stay in a drug rehab centre. The minister's price to pay for everything being swept under the rug would still be unknown.

Mlungisi Radebe

Mlungisi Radebe is an emerging writer from South Africa.

Walking, Falling
Mlungisi Radebe – South Africa

When death blew out my father's candle, my mother was heartbroken. She was numb for weeks, unable to dance to the song of grief. Suicidal thoughts were frequent visitors, hovering on her mind like lovesick dragonflies dancing on a pond.

She was being consumed by sorrows, doing her best not to let go of the worn-out threads of hope. A life without him was too gutting to imagine, frightening as a ghost that sings lullabies to those it haunts. However she prayed, however she fought to break free from the chokehold of grief, sadness seemed to know the perfect places through which to seep in. She, I learned from her deep conversations with God, felt as though she was being punished for loving wholeheartedly. She wore her pain like a dress, one that wasn't long enough to conceal her wounds.

As was customary, she had to remarry in the family. Our tradition says that a widowed woman must not remain widowed when there are unmarried relatives. This is done so the household of the deceased remains safe, so the children grow up having a father figure around. That is the problem with tradition. It is biased, unequal. Elders are the ones who follow ancient ways the most, inviting to critique the way we now do things. They tend to ignore the flow of time, the views that shape this generation. They do things their way, without heeding to the clock whose ticking depicts how we now exist in a different world. Other things, which were relevant centuries ago, no longer have space in this reality that keeps changing its colours like a chameleon in the face of danger.

Mother had no desire for marriage. She merely wanted a job so she'd take care of us. The elders then gave her an ultimatum: if she refused to remarry, she was to leave the house she and my father had built. But she was only young, not stupid. She couldn't force love unwarranted by Cupid, a celestial whose existence no longer meant anything after her husband took earth as a blanket.

Angered by her refusal, the elders wanted us to leave our home. Not only because my mother had refused Kister's proposal – my father's cousin – but because of my father's mistress with whom he had a child. The elders, who were trying to arrange a marriage for her as though she was a piece of property to be passed around, had known of my father's infidelity. Knowing she had us, she stomached all of it: the hate, the disrespect, the shame.

When the elders finally backed off, we lived happily. There was, in our lives, a silence whose weight could be equated with that of a deep breath. Since there was no will, my father's family took his retirement purse, subjecting us to more suffering and destitution. Mother left the house every morning, seeking a job. Her failure to make us look like other children cut her in places her hands could not reach. Being older and wiser, I would ask her to only buy clothes for my younger brother.

To dwindle her suffering, I relocated to Ndwedwe to live with my grandmother. But granny was very sick. She was often hospitalised, leaving me in the care of relatives who kept me detribalised. I went to school barefoot, whilst their children owned extra pairs. At lunch, I would sit alone behind the school lavatories; cursing, cussing, trying to grasp the reason for which God had warranted my existence. My schoolmates always made fun of me, of my old uniform. Everyone picked on me, reducing my self-esteem. Every second I spent breathing felt like a waste of oxygen.

When other kids dreamt of toys, I prayed for an unpatched uniform. When they wanted new clothes, I prayed for shoes with no worn-out heels. At some point, I was sure I would never be happy in this life. The endless bullying broke my spirit, so much that I began contemplating suicide. Some teachers had also come to dislike me, for a reason they kept only to themselves. My own class teacher, Mrs Nkosi, once accused me of stealing her pen. Because I had nothing, not even hope that one day the gods would smile at me.

One afternoon, I stepped on a peel of banana and accidentally broke her glass. She yelled at me, roughly poked my forehead with her index finger. She had witnessed the cause of my fall, my sore thigh but she was never gentle in her scoffs. There was never frailty in her discourse. She called me different, painful names. She made fun of my toes, calling me unworthy of anything. As the other kids laughed at her every affront, I started crying. Repeatedly, she told me to shut up but I couldn't. The tongue has no bones, but it inflicts wounds that never stop bleeding. If, miraculously, they do, they leave excruciating scars. She smacked me for being a cry-baby that my nose began to bleed. Angry that I was making a mess in her polished floor, ruining its fought for shine, she dragged me out of the classroom.

After two long hours, she came with a cane. I was too young to bear that amount of pain, begging for forgiveness after every thrust; hoping she would let go of me. But she never stopped hurting me, I never stopped crying. The other learners were amused by my weeping and screams. My bladder betrayed me, making me wet myself. Only then did she realise that she was hurting me, that what she was doing was wrong. When she let go of me, my whole body was sore. I could not even stand on my feet, so I just laid there... in my urine. Right then, I realised that my grandmother had been delusional to believe there was a caring God.

My cousins, along with their friends, gathered around me. I thought, for once, they'd come in peace, until they started laughing at me. I was numb, emotionless. I wanted to die. Nothing I did was ever right. Then two girls, Thandi and Thando, both of whom were Mrs Nkosi's daughters, helped me to my feet. I got up, slowly, only to realise my left arm had been dislocated. A week later, while I was cleaning the school windows as punishment for sleeping during a lesson, I heard Mrs Nkosi screaming in her office. "Snake! Help! Help!"

Mrs Bhengu rushed to her aid. She screamed as well, darted past me in fear and panic. She said the snake was too big. "You are a boy," she said to me, shaking. "You're used to things of this sort. Please do something, Radebe."

"I'm busy. I have to finish here so I can go home. Find someone else."

"That's not the right way to talk to your teacher, boy."

"It is," I said, shining the window with amazing workmanship, "if she's sending me on a suicide mission."

"Mrs Nkosi might die."

"I have no business meddling with fate. If she dies, it was meant to be. God does not make mistakes."

"Please, Mlungisi."

I went to confront the snake.

It was a green mamba, its body in coils; scary in its emerald hue. It wasn't that big. I took a stick and helped it out of Mrs Nkosi's office. "Kill it!"

"Did it kill you?"

After evicting the snake, I returned to my duties. "You can go home," said Mrs Bhengu, escorting Mrs Nkosi to her car.

Two days later, Mrs Nkosi apologised for all the insults I had to disregard, the piercing scoffs that broke me. Her apology didn't mean anything to me, it carried no weight. It was not enough to make up for the sleepless nights she'd given me, for the tears I'd shed. She had beaten me to a pulp for not raising my hand each time I knew an answer. She had called me all sorts of names for not being able to solve an equation; things other learners did but whom she treated with love and showed the respect a teacher should depict to a pupil. It is unwise to physically punish a child and then seek pardon, cheering them up with gifts to adorn claims of unrequited love. It gives a strange perception of what love is. This would, in the later stages of their lives, lead them into constantly forgiving the people who hurt them. It would blind them from glimpsing the necessity to speak out.

When I turned eleven years old, I had my first friend. From the way he moved his fingers and eyes when saying something, to how he spoke and touched my shoulder whenever I'd said something stupid, I could tell he was different from me and the other boys. Such a quality made us a unique pair: he was bullied emotionally, I was bullied physically. That same year he was burnt alive for being homosexual. Christians killed him, claiming his sexuality was against the laws of nature and an insult to God.

In no time, I reached puberty.

Girls my age loved my curly hair, and the way I performed academically. Mrs Nkosi's daughters were the first to have a crush on me. But my cousins ruined everything by making fun of my worthlessness. Whenever there were people around, they would call me an orphan their parents took in out of pity. They would tell others that the clothes I wore were theirs, that I was a beggar living on handouts.

On one occasion, Minenhle ordered me to take off his shoes while we were at assembly. He was angry that the girl he admired above all else had asked him to tell me she was in love with me. When Mrs Nkosi scolded him, he said I had taken them by force. That same afternoon, while asleep in class, a bucket full of ice cubes was poured over my head. As I had guessed, it was my cousins. I could not take the bullying anymore –

enough was enough. I had run out of patience, of tolerance. I followed the boys, found them in the lavatories.

As I stood by the door, they laughed again. If only they'd heard the strumming of rage echoing within me, the abhorrence that burned in my clenched fists. I locked the door, placed bricks against it to intercept entrance. I took off my shirt, made yellow by dust and rust, and dropped it onto the floor. There were two other boys and both of my cousins, all of whom were laughing at me.

I started with the two boys, putting to use the skills I had obtained from the local boxing club. Then I went to my cousins, beat them to a pulp. Had the principal not come, I am not sure what would have happened. He took me to his office, to talk to me like a father. I asked him to call my mother. I told her about the life I had been living, how I was scared of going back home. She begged the principal to accompany me home, to help pack my belongings.

At Ntwela Junior Primary School, I met Kwanda Shongwe. We became brothers in arms, inseparable. We were frequent guests in the principal's office because of how we always got into fights. At times we'd fight amongst ourselves but would settle our disputes in a matter of minutes. We supported one another in everything, cried together when we were bullied by Mhlengi Mayisela after school. His mother sold the best pies in the hood. She would always put two pies in his lunchbox, for she knew he had a brother. His family was average, neither rich nor poor. Unlike mine as we'd go to bed hungry at times. We would share his money and lunchbox. When mother had received her salary, we'd spend my money. He had a better background; I was feared by every boy in school. No one ever touched him or made fun of his stammers in my presence.

In the fourth grade I met Naledi.

Her fluorescence was kaleidoscopic, her soft gaze seductive and her smile was incredibly beautiful. She became the first beautiful thing to exist in this heart, the light I saw at the end of the tunnel I called a life. She was like a flower from Eden, one that blossomed without water. Looking at her was like staring at a starlit sky while enjoying a glass of wine; it was like seeing a rising sun holding hands with the ocean. Have you ever looked at someone and felt like you're in a reverie? Have you ever looked at someone and found yourself smiling with thoughts that moons knew them by name and that stars were their cousins? The answer was simple for me: Naledi.

She had a flair of perfection, a touch of divinity. I began to understand that I had the flaw of vulnerability, a flaw she made impossible to keep restrained. I loved her crescent moon eyes, how her smile was so refined. Perhaps I was being delusional, but I felt she was an angel pretending to be human. She walked on our school verandas with grace, turning them, as dusty as they were, into her esplanade. To be honest: I was not afraid of confessing my love, of telling her how she lessened pains she never inflicted. I was merely afraid of showing her my scars, of scaring her away with my brokenness. But love kept blossoming, to an extent where I penned a love letter. Naledi wrote a letter back, saying I should come and read my love letter to her. She said she wanted to see me say all the things I wrote. I went to her class, where I read her my letter. To my surprise, she was unmoved. If anything, she seemed confused. That's when I learned that Kwanda had sent my letters to the wrong Naledi. I had to make a decision: exhibit my love anew to the intended or seek pardon to the broken other. I never made a decision until the year ended and we all went to different high schools.

Then mom's boyfriend moved in.

It took us a week to realise he was bad news. He had a drinking problem. On top of that, he had anger management issues. He would spew out a lot of derogatory remarks, before calling my brother and I fatherless bastards. He would come home drunk and start cussing the shit out of everyone. He would grab us by our t-shirts, tell us we had the eyes of killers. Somehow, he was terrified of us, of what we'd become when we grew up. And mother, being a mother, would rush to our aid. Other times he would rearrange her face, claiming an infidelity had occurred in his absence. Seeing mother crying, her face sore and in that state broke me in half. It hardened me, filled my heart with abhorrence and rage. More than anything in this life, I wanted to choke him to death.

I went to school angry. Then Mayisela bullied me, adding to my hatred. I remember telling him to leave Kwanda and I alone, or else I would hurt him. He merely chuckled, vowed that I would pay for that affront after school. I took a brick and hit him, repeatedly. That was the last time he ever touched me. Ironically, my stepdad was the one who came to school to talk to the principal and Mayisela's parents. He sought pardon on my behalf, told the teachers that my anger stemmed from the abuse I had been subjected to in my early years. Upon leaving the principal's office, he praised me for breaking Mayisela's jaw. He said he was proud of me, of how I handled him like a man.

One night, while he was punching my mother, my brother and I took sticks and stones. We'd planned to hurt him the same way he always hurt mom, but he drew out a gun. We ran out crying. I hated myself, I hated being small. Had we been the same age, I would've shown him flames. Boys my age knew I was not someone to mess with. Others, out of fear, chose to stay clear of me. Even when we were caned at school, I'd look the teachers in the eye and not shed a tear or wince in pain. For that reason, my punishments were always severe. I guess I had become accustomed to physical pain. The one thing that left me weak was the sight of my mother's sore face and broken arm. Not being able to deal with my stepdad made me feel small, insignificant.

As fate would have it, he and I met when I was nineteen. Anger got the best of me. I attacked him. We fought and fought and fought. Tired of the fight, perhaps, he took out his gun. He wanted to shoot me, but I was quick to take hold of the gun. I don't remember what happened next, but I did hear a sound. A roar. A groan. Then I saw blood; a lot of it. He collapsed on top of me. He was neither blinking nor moving. I resented him, with every ounce of my being but, in that moment, I wanted him to wake up.

To hit me.

To scold me.

It didn't happen.

Chiedza Nyanyiwa

Chiedza Nyanyiwa is the author of The Covenant of Life and Other Essays. She has loved novels since she read Takadini at the age of twelve. A lover of nature, art and the classics, she finds inspiration for her work in all three. She lives in Harare and has a Master's degree in Child sensitive social policies. When she is not writing or reading, she can be found engaging in her other passion as a child rights practitioner and Children's Republic Association founder.

Facebook: Chiedza Nyanyiwa
Instagram: @chichi_nyanyiwa

The Silence
Chiedza Nyanyiwa – Zimbabwe

The house in which you grew up was small, barely a whisper against the mountain plains that choked your town within its firm and unwavering grip. It stood that house on shaky legs, round with sighed resignation and shaded against the heat by a shabbily thatched roof. You loathed it with a hatred that seemed to have been born with you. Yet in the years to come, each time you closed your eyes as Morpheus took you by the hand and led you to whatever adventures lay in the land he commanded, it was always to that house that he brought you first, as though it were the entrance to your soul, as though it were your beginning and your end. It was small, the house you grew up in. Never big enough to hold your dreams nor your destiny. Never big enough to hold your mother's strength nor the fatalism with which she approached life. Never big enough to contain your siblings' laughter nor tears. Never big enough to hold your father. Yet it stood there, brick tucked besides brick, a fallacy held by the neck by the high mountain plains. The house was a little round thing collapsing from the weight of ill use and no repair, fat from an overconsumption of misery and despair. The misery, of course, was largely due to its own dramatics because your family, regardless of everything, was happy. It was the kind of happiness that came from want, collective want, the kind that looked to eternal things where want and the contentment with it could be rewarded.

They stood there, the mountains, as they had stood when time took its first step and the first stars began to burn in the universe. They stood as they had stood before the land knew its way around the ravines and valleys, and before the oceans learnt to dance to the shores. As the earth blinked to the sun that shined overhead for the first time, the mountains got up from their knees and stood, and there they remained standing, watching as the first of your ancestors crawled from the bosom of the earth from which God had molded them. They watched for thousands and thousands of years as your forefathers' feet gave the earth its identity, the print of its fingers, and taught it to find its way. Yet those same mountains choked you then with the same fingers that had been born of a Word and the eternal breath at the dawn of time. They knew the secrets, those tall mountains, the secret histories of men. And because your house and Shadowville were a lie, a fallacy, they choked you, all of you, with hopes and tears never born, never shed, yet never abandoned.

Shadowville, your village, fell under the shadow of the mountains. The proud mountains howled cold winds that held secrets, only for them to be captured in the empty spaces were the languages they spoke meant nothing to anyone. The tongues, you see, that spoke with them had been cut out centuries before and fed to the gods of history to choke on. These were the same tongues that had taught the roads their ways and given the mountains their names. They had cradled time in their hands and their wombs had given birth to nations before they were ripped from them. They had shown the rivers where to flow and imprinted the earth with their DNA. They had been made from the dust of the earth they stood on before it swallowed them up into an everlasting sleep. It was Shdowville, your mother said, that met at times and in seasons with the silence of God.

It was upon these ancient roads lined with mountains of litter and the repellent perfume of rot that you trudged. You had emerged in the morning from the suffering belly of the ill-used house with a decided purpose in mind. The house had sighed you out, all too happy to suffer in isolation but theatrical as always; it would not spit you out without a clattering and a shaking off of an asbestos and just to make a statement of its own abuse. The purpose of your journey was all but forgotten as soon as your wobbling, protesting feet touched the ground which appeared, with everything else, to protest your existence. The earth, it seemed, had put it in its head that your weight threatened to put a crack on its surface, and so it held you loosely. You thought it dramatic, a wailing monstrosity that had joined with the world in the shunning of all things Shadowville. Still, you challenged it and got on to your business which had neither name nor nature but still had to be got on with, your loose limbs rattling like tin cans in the hands of a child at play.

From her own house by the side of the road, Ms Sanyanga waved at you, a bright smile colouring her mocha face before she raised her winnowing basket, the yellow maize flying in the air with the movement. Clap clap, it rose and fell with the clapping sound that got trapped in your head and refused to escape. The chaff was carried by the winds from the mountains, and in their excitement to be free, filled the air, dancing and swaying from side to side until they were everywhere, too stubborn to come down, those revellers. And so, they followed you, the clapping and the chaff, the earth still reluctant to hold you in its hands.

In a line, the women stood by their doors, cracked and open enough to see the insides labouring at varying degrees as your own was. They waved at you, the women, and at their children in uniforms making their way to those great and exalted places of learning. Well, as it was, you only liked to imagine that these mothers with doeks over their heads, shabby night gowns still on and *zambias* tied loosely around their waists were waving their children away to school. It provided a handsome picture of domestic tranquillity, social harmony, and a splendid vision for the future. The future was dimmed by the chaff that danced and wiggled to the clap clap music of Ms Sanyanga's winnowing labours.

Shadowville had long abandoned the task of sending its children to the great and exalted places of learning. It was not by choice, but the world, it seemed, had a law that balanced the prosperity of Sunville to the regression of Shadowville; the brighter the sun, the bigger the shadow. This law had directed that since the prim and proper children of Sunville needed the latest model of technology, bigger libraries that rivalled the Taj Mahal, larger sporting fields to promote the rounded youths that would one day lead the country, and more nutritious food to make a complete and perfect package of it all, there was simply not enough for the basic facilities demanded by the children of Shadowville. After all, functioning toilets, textbooks, and teachers would be luxuries for children who would grow up to be gardeners and maids for Sunville.

To this grand scheme, Shadowville had laughed. Their children had other designs than those neatly laid out by Sunville. They walked, therefore, through the fog of dancing chaff, moving their feet to the clap clap music of Ms Sanyanga's winnowing, to sit on the waysides, dumpsites, and out of sight, soothed by the magic of booze and marijuana to simulant worlds in which their houses did not suffer from asthma and fits. The more enterprising used the excesses of their energy to stand by the wayside, waiting for detouring cars from Sunvile to pilfer and attempt to bring a sort of balance by redistribution of resources. Others, though, stood by the wayside in tiny skirts and shorts, swaying undeveloped hips in an attempt to catch passersby from Sunville left for them by the Robin Hoods. You passed them, then, on your way to you knew not where, your hands in your pockets, one foot after the other, as you fought with the earth that still complained of failing strength. You knew them by name, the girls. There was Jane, with her large eyes and pink hair, thick lips moving with the well-studied art of gum chewing and popping. She was only twelve years old, and it was with a breaking heart that you recalled, as though it were yesterday, that she had started school, a little playful child that had learnt the alphabet faster than all her peers and come first place in school until the laws of the world had decided against such potential blooming in a place it ought not. Regina, Chipo, Beatrice, Tracie, Rutendo, Rose formed the line with her, Chipo being the oldest at fourteen, and Rose the youngest at eleven. It always surprised you when the men pulled over in posh new cars; big pot-bellied men on their way to give grand speeches on the importance of social inclusion, poverty alleviation, child rights and the classic world peace. Always with unashamed glints in their eyes. Scum of the earth, but it was no use moralising and playing at heroism when the waving mothers had sent their daughters away with smiles and the clap clap sounds of Ms Sanyanga's winnowing. The chaff rolled on with the wind and swept past the girls with a flourish as though determined to outshine them. It swept past them to those lingering about lending their own pattern, to the OOOOOs sifting through the air and puffy clouds of cigarette smoke and marijuana.

It used to be that before everything went topsy-turvy, the men and fathers had respectable occupations. Nothing grand, for as per the design of things, Shadowville had never been made for grandeur. But before the topsy-turvy, when everything was still on its feet and not the other way round, men and fathers had respectable jobs such as carpentering, weaving, driving and some such things. Mothers and women, too, had great industry as weavers, tailors and the like. Those had been the days of domestic tranquillity and social harmony. However, a great recession had hit whose consequences followed the law of the rich getting richer and the poor getting poorer. This recession had cut what little expenditure had been spent on Shadowville, but by some inexplicable turn of things, Sunville's lawns got greener, their houses bigger that they threatened to rival the mountains, their water bluer (if that is in fact the colour of water. Whatever it is, it became more of that), their yards larger and their houses were bellowing boisterous things that grew fat from a diet of contentment, overconsumption and luxury goods. One would be tempted to say they belched from overeating custom paints and expensive carpets, but it can be imagined they were above such vulgar acts.

You stood then, at the edge of Shadowville, looking onto Sunville. A line divided the two towns as though someone had drawn it with a ruler and commanded the shadow not to fall into the light except of course for the provision of menial labour and goods from the vendors' stalls. Behind you, the women, sans night dresses but still in doeks and zambias, set up their stalls and waited for the maids and gardeners from Sunville to cross over to their side. As it was, this too was a fantasy, much like all the hope nursed in Shadowville, for instead of the gardeners and maids, it was the police that came about these days. Vending, they said, was a menace to society that disturbed the beautiful picture presented by Sunville. Thus, more often than not, the women left the edge of town with empty baskets after their lot had been looted, with bruises from baton sticks, hence they sent their children to the waysides, swinging non-existent hips, swinging weapons like Robin Hoods, and puffing their way to dreams and fantasy lands.

With your hands in the pockets of your jeans, you took the first step out of line and the women behind you gasped in surprise. Paying no heed to them, you took a second step forward, and they screamed their protest, but the clap clap of Ms Sanyanga's winnowing was louder than their screams. The chaff, emboldened by your resolve, followed suit and danced its way into the open, perfumed and purified air of Sunville. It did things to your skin, that sun, untainted by smoke and unhindered by mountains. It licked your skin with a warm caress that tingled and awakened in you an ecstasy that travelled through your blood like a drug, and at once, the earth regained enough of its strength to hold you firmly in its palm. You stood upright confidently, a bounce in your stride, as you advanced where your forebears had never dared before. At once, it awakened a recollection of memories hidden in the fog of the morning. You watched, as you advanced with the chaff flying around you, the horrified faces of the men standing next to posh new cars, pot-bellied and in top tier suits, on their way to give grand speeches on the importance of social inclusion, environmental sustainability, poverty alleviation, children's rights and the classic world peace. The women in

Prada, Gucci and Celine gasped their horror, grabbed their children in uniforms on their way to the great and exalted places of learning, and shut their doors behind them, shutting away the horror of so lowly a thing daring to cross to their paradise.

The men advanced towards you, up in arms with bats, guns akimbo, baton sticks ready for an easy kill, but the chaff, angered by this blatant show of disgust and prejudice, scattered like the wind and twirled into a sandstorm. It pushed against them with such force they fell on their backs. It pushed against the windows and locked doors, scattered the expensive Chinese bowls, mahogany tables, the great halls and dining rooms, laying to waste every expense for which Shadowville was sacrificed. It became the wind and carried the rooftops; it danced with the soil and uprooted the manicured lawns. It became an avalanche and buried the town. You, the revolutionary magician, danced to the clap clap music of Ms Sanyanga's winnowing until nothing was left but the men, women and children crying protests against the injustice done to them.

The chaff settled down, giving a bow as it did so. The sun, too, moved from Sunville and hovered over Shadowville. It was such a sight as had never been seen in living memory. It was enough to startle the children by the wayside, those in their stimulant induced stupor, those swaying non-existent hips, and even the Robin Hoods who dropped their weapons of justice. The women abandoned their stalls and the men stopped in their aimless drunken wandering and watched, for the first time, as the sun, in all its golden wonder, washed over them. Your house at the end of the town sighed in great relief for it was quite enough to put it out of its depression, fits, sighs and melancholia. You thought, as you stood there, that without the ruckus of that stubborn and complaining house whose misery was largely its own making, you would be able to at last sleep well at night. With that thought, the earth, that traitorous monstrosity, let go of its hold on you and you collapsed to the ground, the clap clap music of Ms Sanyanga's winnowing echoing still.

Otsile Seakeco

Otsile Sebele Seakeco grew up in Kimberley, in the Northern Cape, South Africa. Added to his love for dogs and fiction, he is a poet interested in creating works of art that enable him to reflect, grapple with, and speak life into the reality of his existence.

Duiffies United VS Di Kwena Mabe

Otsile Seakeco – South Africa

The final fixture had been set. Duiffies United were up against Di Kwena Mabe.

It was incredible to witness how the final fixture of the Coca Cola Cup, the biggest and most contested league in our region, uplifted the community's spirit and transformed its entire atmosphere into something that reflected the warmth and beauty of its people. You could tell in a toddler's laugh, the energy in an Elder's greeting and the amount of smiles you would have to pull, especially when whoever was on the receiving end supported the opposition, that judgement day, as we call it, was upon us.

Unlike other sports, nothing matched the love and support soccer boasted in Tafelsfontein. People discussed the match everywhere you went, and it was known that the street corners, especially the ones closest to the complex, would host the most heated debates. This was also where ideas were shared, where gossip took root and issues related to politics and religion were often discussed. So, whenever I walked past such folk on my way to the shops, I would pass a comment that favoured my team in the middle of such a passionate exchange.

While those in support would normally cheer me on, the opposition, annoyed, would hurl insults at me or my team, then proceed to respond with their thoughts and predictions of the game. The idea was to always brush them off, deflect their remarks and never give them a chance to respond, which I seldom succeeded at.

However, what was more exciting was that my brother, Punch, a nickname he was given after scoring a special goal against their rival team in the 2010 Sunderland Regional Finals, was to play that weekend. I knew my brother was a talented soccer player who worked hard on the field and hated losing, but it was still surprising to learn how he came to earn his nickname.

It is said that Duiffies were trailing by two goals to one when Punch, at sixteen years, was brought on to the field. It was his first time playing in a tournament of that magnitude and against players of that calibre. I am also told that it was his first appearance in front of such a big crowd and that he was put in a position he was recently introduced in to, as a striker, mainly because of his speed and ability to shoot with precision.

"Heh boy, your brother is a brilliant player," a teammate of his relayed to me. "I remember when Coach Zakes asked him to kit up in the changing rooms. We were all surprised at the announcement because we knew how good the opposition was. But we also knew that your brother was just as good, if not better than half of the squad, so that immediately put us at ease. Fifteen minutes into the second half, Coach called him up and the rest was history." He paused for a bit while he grinned, "Do you know what your brother did while we trailed by two goals to one?"

I knew the story. He decided to leave his position as striker to go search for the ball in midfield. When he managed to get it, he dribbled past three players at once then forced a shot at goal. The keeper punched it out to the left side of the field, but my brother quickly closed ground on the player and won the ball. He then passed it to Nguni, who switched it to De Bear. De Bear then managed to find my brother with an excellent through pass. At this stage, everyone was on our feet, Coach didn't know whether to shout at Punch or to encourage him. But in no time, Punch had dribbled past another of their last standing players that had quickly rushed back to defend their goal. The opposition coach, realising what was unfolding, kept shouting at his goalkeeper to punch the ball out of goal, when my brother unleashed a powerful shot.

"Punch! Punch! Punch the ball out of goal," he kept shouting, but unfortunately, his cries were not enough to save their team or the keeper from my brother's tenacious strike. They went on to win that match by three goals to two, and it was from that day that everyone started calling him Punch, in celebration of not only aiding his team to such a memorable victory but to also mock the opposition's goalkeeper and coach.

We had a good laugh about it, the week progressed, and everyone kept talking about the big game. I smiled and pictured myself wearing my brother's jersey number 10 and seeing him do wonders on the pitch. He had left home for the entire week to prepare for the final, leaving me with no opportunity to see or talk to him before the match.

I remember waking up much earlier that Saturday morning to help my mother with the chores. It was a bit difficult for me to do everything around the house by myself with mom's ageing, my sister's matrimony and with my brother hardly home. It was overwhelming and frustrating at times to work the garden, tend to the chickens and feed the other animals, but the thought of walking Desiree to the match overturned my fatigue.

I looked forward to hearing what her predictions were and to get her opinion on some of the key players' performances in recent games. She was ahead and more knowledgeable about soccer than most of us, and it was certainly true when the older boys poked fun at us when her skills surpassed ours, that she was better than many of us. I found her standing in front of their house, talking to her mother and aunt over the fence.

The walk to the grounds was long and tiring, however, witnessing Punch's first touch on the ball was welcoming enough to find us in sync with the crowd. It was perfect, if not magical.

The sky was beautifully clear and the sun, comfortably warm. People from neighbouring villages as far as twenty kilometres away came in their numbers to watch the match and to support their team. I heard a lot of people cheer my brother on, especially when he went up against Kristi, one of the best soccer players in our region. Just like my brother, he started playing for Di Kwena Mabe from a very young age and was the breath of brilliance and jewel everyone from Gatlose took pride in.

The match was electrifying, and the two teams had a substantial go at each other. There was a lot of drama towards the end of the match when players constantly played foul, the referee was accused of favouritism and players would keep to one or two touches as opposed to showcasing their skills. The game was very entertaining and intense, but one moment stood out for me. This was probably around the eightieth minute when Punch received the ball on the touch line.

His reception was excellent, and so was his second touch. He played it to Skara, but Skara was soon intercepted by Kristi who played the ball to one of his teammates. He then played the ball into the middle of the field where he received it back, and just when he was about to switch it to the left-hand side of the pitch, a stone plunged onto his head.

No one knew where it came from and where it ended up. One thing was certain though, a stone hit the player, and he instantly fell to the ground. Desiree was dumbstruck; the look on her face captured the shock and disbelief on everyone's faces. The match was stopped for a few minutes while everyone, including the two teams, looked for the stone, but no one found it. Both coaches did a sterling job to manage the crowd and their players to restore order.

The player was eventually substituted, and the match resumed. The match went into extra-time and then penalties, and for the first time in three or four years, Di Kwena Mabe took the glory. They won the penalty shootout by five goals to three. I walked home disappointed and sad but had Ma to cheer me up.

The next morning, Mama and I were surprised to see two big vehicles parked in front of our homestead. One was plain white, and the other was covered in blue, black, and red. A short white man emerged from the white vehicle and asked me, "Bly Punch hier so?" Does Punch live here?

To which I replied, "Ja." Ma immediately questioned if Punch had fallen victim to some form of tragedy, an accident, but the other man that followed, a fairly built, middle-aged Indian man smiled and said no. Punch was fine, and they were here to talk to his mother.

"I am his mother," my mom replied. They proceeded to talk under our big tree, which serves as a veranda.

It was only after they had left that I learnt the two men were underdevelopment scouts from a popular football team in Johannesburg, Gauteng. A place many in my village feared and admired in equal measure because, as they said, it was the capital where freedom was bought with the size of your pocket. Being quite young at the time and never having left our province, I was fascinated by why they would want to take Punch away from a community that loved him so much, let alone from us, his family. I was equally stunned to see how the two men begged my mother to grant Punch the permission to go to trials in Johannesburg.

The other people in the two vehicles seemed reserved and uninterested; they looked like soccer players themselves but a bit older than Punch. Out of curiosity, I went closer to the bigger of the two vehicles. It intrigued me because everyone in it seemed to have something plugged in their ears. It was only later in life that I found out they were earphones. I asked the one closest to the door where they were taking my brother. He took his earphones off to ask if I could repeat myself. I did, then he said, "Don't worry, your brother won't make it there, so he'll be back soon." I was taken aback by his cold demeaner but soon brushed it off after he gave me a R50 when I had asked for a R5. I was happy and thought maybe it was not such a bad idea for my brother to go to the trials.

Punch was home late the next day with Coach. He knew the two men had paid mother a visit to ask if he could go to the trials. Coach, with a stern look on his face, sat there while I went back and forth to pour him cool drinks. His voice irritated me, but I admired his relationship with Punch – the two were inseparable. Punch always said how his talent meant very little without Coach's grooming. When this thought came to mind, I dragged myself to pour him what I had already determined would be his last glass.

At the end of the day, it was resolved that Punch would go to the trials. This was after a series of deliberations that eventually convinced my mother. It was sad news for me; however I was excited for him. He wouldn't stop talking about how he could be promoted to the first team in two years which he deemed quite achievable. We spoke right into the early hours of the morning while he packed his belongings.

A week after his departure, Punch called on Jeffrou Duiker's phone to inform us that he had made it through the trials. The Duikers were one of the few families that owned a mini tuckshop in our village. We were all excited and happy for him. But the thought of having to do everything on my own around the house devastated me until Punch asked Ma to give me pocket money. It was tough at first, but I managed because the workload lessened since we could afford to buy some of the produce we relied on from our animals and garden.

It was a year now since Punch had left home and everywhere I went, people sought after his well-being. His first visit home came with t-shirts, tracksuits, and bags from his team which he gave to me, Desiree, and my cousins. We were so proud of him and everyone in my village held him in the highest regard. In a period of two years, he had bought us a flat screen television where we'd get to see him play and invite others to watch. We built a house out of the fanciest bricks that have travelled this far, with a satellite dish where mother's friends usually resigned to enjoy Africa Magic.

Everything was perfect. I had finally made it to matric after repeating grade eleven. Then we learnt that Punch had picked up an injury that would put him on the bench for about six months. At first, it didn't bother me much, until he came home to start living with us. Everywhere he went, people asked for an explanation, and I could see how this got to him. One rainy night in winter, he called me to his room and asked me to make him a hot cup of coffee.

He called me back just when I was about to leave the room. I turned back, thinking he was about to reprimand me for coming home late the previous night, but instead, he expressed his gratitude towards me for having held the fort while he was away. "Mother is proud of the young man you've become. None of us escape her praises, but she is extremely proud of how you bounced back from repeating grade eleven. So are myself and your sister. While in Johannesburg, I met a lot of people who opened me up to different worlds and experiences. Most were life-changing and inspiring, while others became real and tough life lessons. One of my teammates advised me to open a savings account for your studies. I only managed to secure an amount that will cover your first year, which means you will have to work hard to obtain a bursary afterwards. I have also spoken to a few resourceful people to assist you, but I don't want us to put too much faith in them. Contrary to what we are often told, the world owes you a lot, but unfortunately, it is not prepared to recognise or come to terms with that. Until a better world is fashioned and there are better and more opportunities for a meaningful existence for people like us, we need to treat life and the world as if it owes us nothing while we use what we achieve and who we become as a contribution to creating a better world. As you know, my plans and ambitions have been gravely affected by my injury. I am not sure how long it will take for me to recover without the support of proper facilities and professional guidance. My agent called me the other day to tell me that the club has bought two additional players that play in my position and were reluctant to disclose if my contract would be extended."

I didn't know what to say. I wondered if my brother could be treated with a little bit more compassion. I felt hatred overcome me, because unlike similar cases I had heard of before, this involved my brother, my hero. What also pained me was that until today, Punch had hardly spoken about the one thing he loved and lived for. This broke me. The next months proved to be even more challenging for him, especially when one prominent sport analysist mentioned that it was unlikely that his contract would be extended.

It was tough seeing Punch slowly lose hope. His drinking escalated to every weekend and hosting parties every month-end became him and Ma's quarrel. I wondered what life had in store for him if he did not get to play soccer again or discover something else that he could live for.

I had just matriculated with three distinctions and an average that exceeded my expectations. My departure for university was exciting and emotional. Since childhood, I had feared and dreamt of seeing the world beyond Tafelsfontein. I believe my mother and immediate family shared the same sentiment. Their love and well wishes accompanied me to the bus stop with strong reiterations of their sound and funny advice, warm hugs and where there was, several pennies were secretly passed to me.

The back seat I occupied in the bus gave me a decent view of the beauty and squalor that still welcomes me to many cities. It was also the window through which I followed the artwork on tall, beautiful buildings, the specular glass on others and most intriguing, the cars that drove past us, together with the pedestrians that swamped the streets. Their movement suggested the culmination of many stories unfolding, others half-way, a few accomplished, and most largely dreadful.

I drew conclusions about who did what while I looked on with curiosity at the pace and expressions many held. Without losing sight of all the dangers I was warned about, I wondered how my story would take shape. Would it resemble the most attractive or the worst figures I lent my eyes and imagination to? It was in that moment that I resolved and pledged to fight and live for my dreams.

This was true until my new life found me abhor the dreams I once harboured and made me feel a certain kind of betrayal towards those who had helped instil them in me. I had set plenty of goals for myself coming to the city, nothing close to the number Punch had scored of course. However, discovering that the world I inhabit was largely built for my detriment, I rallied behind the ideas and words of individuals whose lives had been devoted to what my brother echoed about fashioning a better and meaningful existence for people like us, and most importantly, who ensured that we knew that contrary to what the world says, it does, in fact, owe us a lot.

Flora Chikasha

Flora Chikasha is a Zimbabwean short story writer with a legal
background. Gethsemane is her first published short story

Gethsemane
Flora Chikasha – Zimbabwe

I didn't know it yet, but I entered the Garden of Gethsemane when I was on the specialist's table having a scan. I already knew things were not good; I had a sense of anxious foreboding before I stepped into the room. The Gates of Gethsemane slipped shut without me knowing and I was unaware they would hold me there. My heart was beating fast, and my breathing was shallow as I lay on the examination table. It was covered with a green cotton sheet and smaller, pink, cotton head and foot sheets.

I was told to cover my lower half with a pink cotton sheath. I raised my tunic, and a large piece of tissue was stuffed into the top of my pants. I waited for two lifetimes back-to-back, it seemed, before the familiar cold gel touched my skin and the doctor's ultrasound tool began its work. I glanced at the monitor and then immediately looked away again. I couldn't bear to look.

Mudiwa, my husband, was standing nearby, clutching my legs firmly but warily, a kindly, steady and solemn expression on his dark, handsome but care-worn face. There was absolute silence for a few moments as we tried to decipher the strange shadows we saw on the monitor. I could hear my heart beating and my rapid breaths, like the panting of an impala that's been running from a lion, that desperately needs to take a break to get its breath back, but knows its time is up. Ridiculously, I was embarrassed by these noises and tried to slow down my breathing by taking one deep breath and exhaling slowly. It seemed to help.

I am not sure who spoke first, the specialist doctor, or Mudiwa, to ask him what was going on.

"It's fourteen weeks," said the doctor slowly. Then, "Heartbeat. There."

I saw some movement on the screen and Mudiwa and I both smiled briefly, nervously.

"It's moving," He added, referring overall to the foetus.

We could see something like arms and legs, moving in a sort of swimming motion. I wondered if foetuses were amphibians before they were born? How else could they survive in fluid for nine months without drowning? How did they breathe?

We nodded at the specialist doctor's comments. We knew they were just icebreakers. We wanted to know more about what had been hinted to us in the two previous scans, that there was some "slight cranial distortion" and about the apparent cyst on the top of the baby's head. We saw it immediately, the bubble on top that looked like a space helmet. We had seen it before, too, in other scans. Today, the helmet seemed to be reflecting light so that it looked as if it were made of glass. It looked unique, almost creative, like something Lady Gaga or the late Michael Jackson would have come up with as part a stage performance costume.

"You know about the fibroid?" the doctor asked, picking up a small, dark, immobile shadow lower down.

"Yes, yes. It's not dangerous, is it?" Mudiwa responded.

The doctor replied briefly "No, no." Then he homed in on the cyst, the bubble helmet. "This is not good."

"What do you mean?"

"Hmmm… unfortunately, it is really not good. The foetus has some severe distortions in the cranial region…"

"Go on," Mudiwa prompted him.

"You see, the skull is completely absent…"

At that point, without thinking, I covered my eyes with my hands and drew in a sharp breath. From that moment on, I felt as though I was drowning in a deep, dark pool of something murky and cold, that everything that was being said was sinister and threatening, and that whatever was taking place was happening far, far, away. I didn't want to hear more. I wanted to jump up and run away. I was no longer looking at the screen. I couldn't.

I kept my eyes covered and instantly felt them fill with tears. My breaths were now sobs and I was helplessly whispering "No! No!"

It's all I could do.

The doctor pressed on, "…The skull is completely absent and there is only fluid, which is held only by a membrane. That's the membrane that appears to be filled with fluid. Can you see it?"

Mudiwa answered, "Oh no… Oh my God. Yes. I can see it. The bubble… Is it dangerous? Is the baby is going to be alright?"

The Doctor responded sadly, quietly but clinically "I'm afraid not. This condition is fatal. The baby is not going to make it."

He might as well have thumped me on the side of the head with a hammer or a brick. The pain was instant and intense. It was not a physical pain but a mental and emotional one. I sobbed louder, a cry of anguish that seemed to be coming from someone else. The irrational thought that came to me at that moment, as if from a casual spectator watching a play unfold on the stage before them, was *How appropriate, I am dressed in black today.*

My nose was full of mucus and tears were rolling down my face. I was wailing as the examination ended, and I raised myself off the clinical bed, slowly and stiffly as Frankenstein's monster rising from his Master's table and wiped my tummy before lowering my knee-length black maternity tunic over my black leggings. I simply could not believe what I had heard. I wanted to un-hear it. I did not want to believe it. I did not want to be there. I wanted to run away. But the doctor kindly drew us to his table to explain further, and he offered to immediately call our gynaecologist, Dr. Mandiziva, with the diagnosis. He checked something carefully in a big textbook on his desk before gently explaining to us in a kind voice that the condition was called *anencephaly.* That this was a severe case of anencephaly, which was linked to and could also be referred to as *acrania.* It was an extremely rare condition that only affected one in twenty thousand mothers. Basically, the neural tube failed to close at the right time of the child's development, leaving its brain exposed. The foetus was probably only alive because of the membrane containing the fluid – water, apparently – covering whatever matter remained in the cranial cavity.

"The foetus cannot survive. Your body, which does not like something which is abnormal, might reject it. When that happens, the foetus will be spontaneously expelled from the body. In other words, there is a slight possibility that you will miscarry." He softly added, almost to himself, glancing down at the textbook over his spectacles, "I am actually surprised that this one has made it so long and seems to be moving so actively."

He went on in a more official voice, "If you don't miscarry, and the foetus grows to full term, it will most likely be a still birth. As soon as you go into labour, the contractions of your uterus will start to squeeze the baby. And because it has no skull, the baby's head will be crushed. There is an almost zero percent chance that it will survive delivery. And even if it does, it will only live for moments, maybe for a few hours or a day or so at most, before it dies."

Mudiwa mentioned the fact that Tawa, our first child, aged thirteen, was on the autism spectrum. The specialist doctor was of course aware that autism was a special-needs condition that affected the speech, social development and behaviour of a child, that such children could grow up with no speech and display unusual and repetitive behaviours such as constant rocking, finger-twirling, head banging or hand-flapping. Tawa was, in fact, severely autistic.

"Oh," the doctor looked at us, surprised, sympathetic. "How much care does Tawa need, from day to day?" We explained to the doctor Tawa's condition. That he was completely non-verbal, needed help with day-to-day processes like feeding, and was still in diapers. We told him about Tawa's hidden creative talent and obscure intelligence, his ability to compose and tap out various rhythms and even to make up a tune on the piano, playing with both hands the very first time we ever witnessed him do so, on the piano at Heathrow Airport, an installation artwork marked *"Play Me."* Mudiwa had a video clip of the event on his cell phone. The doctor asked if we had any other children and we told him about Pippitto, our eleven-year-old foster son, whom we had met in the rural areas years ago, when he had lost his parents at the age of four. A good boy. The doctor nodded sympathetically, as if considering why such bad things had to happen to apparently good people like us.

I wept on and on through all of this. The large piece of tissue that had been tucked into my pants during the examination now became my hanky, mopping up the deep stream of tears and mucus flowing relentlessly down my face. I needed to urinate and told the specialist doctor so. He arranged for me to be escorted to the ladies' toilet by one of the nurses

I was grateful to go, and while I was out of the room, he made the necessary phone call to the gynaecologist.

When I returned to the room, he was still on the phone with her. I overheard a snatch of his advice, "…this condition carries a 100% mortality rate… Yes. That's right. It's 100% lethal…"

I almost bolted straight back out of the room, but I could not as the sister clumsily and unintentionally blocked my way, and Mudiwa beckoned me back into the office. I trudged in, hangdog, like a condemned man on death row going to face his final punishment.

The specialist doctor concluded his telephone conversation with the gynaecologist, hung up and rested his elbows carefully on the table, steepling his fingers before him authoritatively.

"Basically," he said, never deterring from his professional, kindly tone, "You have choices. You can choose to legally terminate the pregnancy…"

I wailed and buried my face in my paper hanky.

"… in which case," he continued, "there will be forms for you to fill in. I will sign, your gynae will sign, they will be sent to the Ministry of Health and Child Welfare. Usually, the response takes no more than about two days."

He paused briefly, allowing us to take in what he had just said, then continued, "Of course, the choice is yours, not the medical practitioners'. We will respect whatever your wishes are."

We both nodded silently. We were both shell-shocked.

The doctor gave us a little more advice, assurance that this had come about not as a result of anything the mother had or hadn't done – it just happened. No one knew the cause of this type of condition other than that it was caused, possibly, by some vague combination of genetics and environmental factors. It was in no way connected to Tawa's autism, and in fact was far, far less common than autism; that the possibility of this condition recurring was miniscule, he had never known it to happen a second time round to the same person; and that next time, we needed to be aware that we should take folic acid well in advance of the pregnancy. That we could try again. Maybe as soon as three months after…

"I will write a letter now for the sisters to type, and you can take it back to your gynae right away. Then you can take it from there," he concluded and got down to the business of writing his brief report to which he attached a snapshot from the scan. How could anyone tell what was going on by looking at that scan? All I could see were vague shadows. Perhaps he was mistaken. Perhaps we needed another opinion. Perhaps this whole episode was just a huge misunderstanding.

But even as these thoughts were running through my mind, I heard myself and Mudiwa politely saying, "Thank you so much Doctor."

And I could hear far, far away, the specialist doctor's concluding remarks, his professional manners impeccable to the very end, "I hope we can meet again in better circumstances."

Whatever happened after that, for the rest of the day, was unclear. I know we didn't see the gynaecologist right away because we didn't have the money yet to pay for the consultation and be able to claim it back from medical aid. My salary hadn't yet gone in. I know we went home; going to the office was out of the question. I remember talking to my parents on the phone, and I could hardly speak as I was crying and sobbing so hard. When I walked, it was at the bottom of a dark, noiseless ocean. I was enveloped in a dark, heavy cloud, as deep and lethal as squid ink. I ate little, but my body, despite everything, demanded some nourishment. The baby, alive and active, demanded it. It was the last meal of a doomed man on death row.

Even if the wretched man orders the most delicious burger and ice cream and soda as his last meal on earth, does he taste it? I cannot recall what I ate – that meal may as well have been cardboard washed down with liquid nitrogen.

I thought of millions of things. All my thoughts were fragmented, shooting through my mind like arrows at the speed of light. I struggled to latch onto them, they slipped through my conscience so fast I could barely make sense of them. Nothing was logical, nothing was rational. I thought of the coincidence of the baby's due date, which we had been advised would fall somewhere between the 22nd and the 28th of May 2014, with my own birthday falling on the 24th of the same month. I saw images of the pram, the cot and the Moses crib we had bought only weeks before. I thought of our agreed plan to buy something each month in preparation for the baby's arrival: this month, it was meant to be the baby's bathtub. I thought of the baby clothes we had bought, the little baby growers, the baby gowns, and the little baby socks cleverly designed to look like tennis shoes. I imagined that the foetus was a boy. I was convinced it was a boy.

I sat down in front of my husband's computer and googled *Anencephaly* and *Acrania* and immediately, was assaulted by cruel, harmful, unforgiving words and images. Babies with half a head.

Foetuses, orange-skinned, dead, with bulging eyes and the top of the head missing. Cold, heartless, clinical write-ups. Everything the doctor had told us was confirmed. No chance of survival. *Not compatible with life.* No brain. Deaf, blind, if it survives delivery and childbirth it may die within hours or at most a few days.

I screamed at the internet.

Mudiwa told me not to look any more.

I can remember, as if observing it in a dream, an image of myself lying down on my bed. I didn't know whether I had crawled or floated up the stairs. I recall not being able to rest, not even to read fiction as I always do to relax. The thoughts kept coming and coming, and so did the tears.

Distraught, I thought of myself ending my little baby's life. In my mind, a knife was handed to me. An echoing, perfectly reasonable, kind and polite voice said *"Here. Take it. It's perfectly in order, you know. We have signed the forms. It's perfectly legal. It's not your fault."*

Next, my mind filled with a different image, one of me suddenly finding blood in my pants and rushing to the toilet, only to find great clots of blood and flesh following uncontrollably before I could do anything to hold it in check. A different, but equally kindly, sympathetic voice came to me, *"It's not your fault my dear. These things happen. Nothing you could have done to stop it happening. What you need right now, my dear, are maternal pads. Hospital quality. With loops."*

Then this vision changed without warning, and I saw myself growing big, bigger, then huge, fourteen weeks melting into six months, eight months, then nine months, as if by time-lapse photography. The baby now full-term, the baby boy with a bubble helmet, the helmet bursting with the pressure, the amniotic fluid of the womb now a poison flowing where it should not go, my baby's life being ended cruelly and mercilessly by my own body, slowly, firmly, harshly, rhythmically, relentlessly squeezing the precious life out of its innocent little body, crushing its poor little head.

I saw images of my newborn's face, with bulging eyes and only the bottom half of its face; nothing from the forehead up. I longed to hold this baby in my arms, to kiss its peaceful face, yet I feared it at the same time, and I wanted to run away from its image in fear and denial. I screamed silently as the tears flowed and my heart and head seemed to burst wide open.

Fourteen weeks. I loved my baby. We both loved the baby, even though we did not yet know if it was a boy or a girl.

And yet, this was not the end. As I was drawn further into my own personal Gethsemane, my anguish and distress were yet to deepen and become more profound.

The agony in the garden grew deeper, not with the madness of the images in my inner mind, but with the conversations. The conversations between us and the small circle of people who knew I was expecting. We had not announced my pregnancy widely among family and friends. We had told our parents and selected siblings, and some very close friends, but not aunts, uncles and acquaintances. Most of the extended family members were not aware. So these conversations took place between Mudiwa and me, me and my parents, me and my mother-in-law, Mudiwa and his mum, his brother, me and Mudiwa's cousin. The gravity and pain of the decision that would have to be made became more poignant and more difficult with each dialogue.

Mudiwa was adamant that I keep the baby. Let it grow to full term, have the baby, and trust everything to God.

"I strongly believe that with God, anything is possible. A miracle is possible. With prayer, and with God, it is possible for the child to come out normal and go on to lead a normal life. This is the time for God to show His power!"

We found that this view was repeated in various formats and different words through the mouths and hearts of others. Young, pretty Tete Anne, who came into my room in the evening, who fell to the floor and wept for me and my baby when she heard the news, who went on to give a confident and spirit-filled testimony in bold, rounded words, before gushing out a series of powerful and passionate prayers, that lapsed into prayers in tongues. My Dad, who gave the staunch Catholic view over the phone, calling from England, that I should *not* end the life of the unborn baby. That such a decision should be left in God's hands. The role of the medical practitioners should be to preserve life, not to tell us to end it. They should do their best to save the life of *both* the mother and the baby. We should be firm with them and tell them that. My cousin Mercy, who, via prolonged conversations on WhatsApp, shared my anguish, having been a mother of a beloved special needs child herself, the child having passed away as a teenager. Mercy, at first, said she would stand by whatever decision I would make. But later, she gave a firm, clear view, that I should keep my baby. Pray for a miracle, have faith. The baby would be a testimony to faith. My sister, Mary, who said she could completely understand the distress I was in and the dilemma of having to make such a terrible choice.

But my mother-in-law came to see me quietly, and mother-to-mother, woman-to-woman, she shared with me the sad and traumatic story of her own loss in the years before she had my husband Mudiwa, her last child. She had had a stillbirth, and it had been the most painful experience of her life.

She had given birth to a very large baby and the nurses had refused to show her the baby. But she had insisted against the nurses' wishes and seen the huge head, the large, lifeless body. She advised me not to go through what she had gone through. There was no point in going through all that suffering, when I knew already that there was no hope the baby would live. She had waited six years after her gruesome ordeal, before trying again for a baby for the last time, with Mudiwa. *Mudiwa.* You are loved, she had named him, her last child.

But I didn't have six years. I was already forty-one years old, and we were already trying for our last-chance baby. We had been so happy, so delighted, so filled with hope when we had confirmed the pregnancy while visiting my parents weeks earlier. I had done everything I had been meant to, from the minute I found out I was pregnant: immediately stopped all medications, alcoholic and caffeine-based drinks, purchased pregnancy supplements, Bio-oil and stretchmark creams, adopted a healthy diet abundant in fresh fruits and green vegetables. I had even stopped taking any other supplements or using any cosmetics for my own vanity, such as the hair, skin and nail supplements and any superfluous face creams. I found I didn't need any of that anyway, as my skin developed a beautiful, smooth, glowing complexion on its own, and my hair flourished naturally. I did away with weaves and wore my hair naturally. I wore flat shoes and selected a few pregnancy outfits I would feel comfortable in at work and at home. I found I needed them fairly soon as I gained weight almost instantly after stopping my blood-pressure control medication. My face grew puffed and bloated and my feet, legs and hips filled with water. My breasts puffed themselves out proudly, straining at my bra. Anyone who knew me and saw the change in my physical appearance put it down to ordinary weight-gain. We let only those closest to us in on the secret: that it was not just weight gain but also massive water retention in my early pregnancy. Tete Anne and my mum in law were discreetly delighted at the news of the pregnancy.

***

I don't have six years to play around with. You see, I am almost at the end of my fertile life as a woman. I am on the last train ride of my fertility. And we need to have this baby. Having a baby means the world to us. It has brought us closer together, Mudiwa and me, as husband and wife, as we've been bonded by the experience. It has led us to prayers together, thanking God for the precious gift of new life. It means that apart from Pippitto, Tawa will have a real blood brother or sister who will be able to look out for him when we are gone. And anyway, I've regretfully put off having a second biological child for most of our thirteen-year-old marriage for the sake of my once soaring career, that has come to not much at the end of it all. When everything else has been taken into perspective, the gift of new life, the gift of love, seems to matter so much more than anything else in this world. And though we are not rich and only earn a modest income, God has taken care of all our needs so far, so we trust it will continue to be possible for us to care for this child.

In my troubled mind, the emerging, growing and fading images of the baby, of abortion, of miscarriage, of stillbirth and of the gruesome, fearful sight of my newborn baby slip away like shadows in the night and are replaced by numbers, mathematics and logic. I am forty-one. I would be forty-two years old by the time the baby arrives. If the baby would live, I would be fifty-two by the time the child is ten. And Tawa would be twenty-three by then, and still non-verbal, still needing to have his diapers changed, still having to take epilepsy medication three times a day – maybe more by then. By the time the new baby is grown to the age of eighteen, I would be sixty years old. An old lady, ready to retire. Would the new child fend for himself by then? Or would I have to sell everything I owned to put him through college? And still, I would be caring for Tawa. Our project, for the establishment of a learning and therapy centre for children with autism in Zimbabwe, had not taken off yet, but was still close to my heart. Would I have achieved that dream by

164

then? And what would Mudiwa have achieved as the father of these children? He gave up his own career for the sake of mine. And now, we are at the mercy of the Zimbabwean environment. Trying to hustle and make ends meet like everyone else. Will he have a viable business enterprise up and running by then, and be able to sustain the family? Will I be able to sit back, relax and simply be a mother?

The numbers and the scenarios fade away and once again are replaced by the torment and the bizarre contradictions of the dialogues we are going through.

There are no guiding principles. Everything is the right choice, everything is the wrong choice. The men join forces and rally together: fathers, brothers, husbands, the Catholic Church. *She must go through with it, no matter what. We don't believe in taking the life of the unborn child in your own hands. Let man be man and God be God. Let man not play God. Let God's will prevail.* The women – mothers and sisters – sympathetically link hands and whisper words of comfort in my ear. *It's you, the woman, the mother, that has to go through with this – is it worth it? I don't want to see you suffer, my dear. Just end it now and forget about it, try again. Next time will be so much better. Take it easy, give it a bit of time. Next time, it will definitely work out alright.* The Doctors, the atheists and the pragmatists give us the scientific facts, and the practical way forward, straight up. *Here are the facts. Here are the forms. Don't over-complicate things. There is absolutely no way this baby can survive. We will help you. You don't have to hold the knife yourself – we will hold it for you… Actually, its not a knife at all; it's just a little poison and your womb will open up, baby comes out, the hospital will deal with it, your womb will be cleaned out, it will be as if nothing ever happened, then you can move on with your life and start all over again.*

And who am I? What am I? I am the mother. I have the power to make a choice. But I am, first and foremost, the host for this growing, fragile unit of life, this force of nature. I have long since told myself that I am just the host.

I am just the house in which this baby will live and grow until it's time to be let out into the fresh air. My job is to make life as comfortable and as safe as possible for this growing entity, this undefined human being. Am I to end it?

Tawa walks into the room as I am sitting on the side of the bed, a shawl wrapped around my shoulders. My head is lowered, my lips cracked and puffy, my eyes swollen from crying all night and day. Curtains are drawn. All is dull and dark, reflecting the state of my mind and of my soul. I see Tawa's innocent eyes and my heart lifts for a moment as his presence in the room makes me feel better for a moment. I see his wide-spaced eyes and his beautiful heart-shaped face. Tawa quietly walks towards me and sits next to me. His small, thirteen-year-old, inquisitive and intelligent hand rests lightly on my shawl, then he pulls the shawl open, revealing my maternity t-shirt that covers my ample breasts and protruding belly. His lips don't move, he makes no sound. His silent, innocent eyes hold one simple question. *What's in there, Mummy?*

I don't answer and I don't see Tawa leave the room. But he does. And all is dark once again.

My night in Gethsemane is long. Life goes on as before. I pull on my work clothes and go to the office and work through my files and in my free time, listen to Andrea Boccelli Oliver Mtukudzi, Tocky Vibes. I read and cook meals, bathe and take my pregnancy supplements and feel the baby moving and kicking. I take morning walks with Mudiwa and spend long nights reading about autism and anencephaly and acrania on the internet. And I cry myself to sleep, exhausted, at night and wake up in the morning, my breasts and belly ever bigger than the day before.

But in my parallel existence, I go on and on in my agony in the garden and the night continues to envelop me with its suffocating cloud of darkness. The answer does not come. The Gates of Gethsemane continue to hold and contain me. No sign comes, no revelation reveals itself to me, no inspiration, no clear directional decision without the harsh consequences of judgment, regret and remorse. Innocent eyes haunt me. They ask the silent question. "What's in there, Mummy?" There is no answer. There is no closure. This night, my night in Gethsemane, goes on and on.

Takomborerwa Shenje

Takomborerwa Shenje is a Zimbabwean writer born in Bulawayo. She captures the kaleidoscope of being an African woman in a globalised heartbeat. She mainly writes about love, loss, identity, and what it means to be a woman in this contemporary climate. Her works include short stories, and an online blog where she writes about her personal observations and struggles.

But Takomborerwa isn't just mourning – she's celebrating. Her stories sing with the vibrant music of youth, the laughter that ripples through crowded kitchens, and the unyielding spirit that pushes through concrete and doubt. She reminds us that even in the cracks of hardship, beauty blooms, resilience takes root, and love defies definition.

Her social media handles are:

Substack: spiritualspinster.substack.com

Bblogspot: takowrites.blogspot.com

God's Country
Takomborerwa Shenje – Zimbabwe

It was a long trek from the local shops where we had parked the car to my paternal rural home. Barefooted children had paused their afternoon play to stare curiously at us, their wire cars and mud houses abandoned in the dust. We were deep in the mountains, and Mozambique lay ahead, unseen in the distance.

The hills and mountains rolled one into the other in a dizzying repetition, giant masses of greens, greys and blues. The mountains were covered in thick, dense foliage, the only breaks in this vast green landscape coming from homesteads and the red and brown earth of dust roads. The air up there was crisp, and I could already feel my tired, sluggish body, weighed down from breathing in the smoky city air, start to slowly be rejuvenated.

Next to me, Junior stretched, already looking more alive than I had ever seen him. That was the effect that Vhumbunu had on people: it revived. There was only one shop back then, an ancient little store called a 'General Dealer's' with a shabby, peeling mahogany exterior and that sold all sorts: warm bottles of coke, soap, cooking oil, shoes… That was where we would do the grocery shopping. The store was owned by distant relatives – around there I was related somehow to almost everyone – and graciously, they had allowed us to park our car there for the duration of our trip while we walked the rest of the way.

Junior had never been there before, and like a child, his head whipped back and forth outside the shop's front door as he tried to take everything in . The beauty of the place was astounding. It was midafternoon, and although it was summer, the air was cool. There was a limited choice of groceries, so I only bought the essentials. We could have done the shopping in Mutare, but I had decided against it, deciding to line my relatives' pockets instead. Some sense of clan loyalty that had been passed onto me by my parents.

The shopkeeper asked about the welfare of my family, who, for the first time, I had travelled there without, though her eyes kept darting to Junior in the doorframe. She was a small and stooped old woman. I wasn't sure how to introduce him yet. We were not married, not engaged, and in my culture, it is difficult to explain the concept of a boyfriend. I told her he was a family friend, which was not really a lie. Begrudgingly, I called him over to introduce himself. In broken Shona, he told her it was lovely to meet her, and I could see she was puzzled by the sight of a black man whose mouth tripped over his own tongue.

"What did you introduce me as?" he asked me. Junior barely understood Shona, let alone a word of my rapid chiManyika exchange with the shopkeeper.

I lied. "I told her we're engaged." He frowned at that.

Groceries packed securely in plastic bags, we hauled out the rest of our luggage, locked the car and set off. We'd tried to pack the necessities. It would be a long walk, somewhat of a hike, and weighing ourselves down with unnecessary luggage would only make us slower. In a show of hospitality, some of our luggage had already been carried off by some adolescent boys, whom I'm sure I was also related to. Soon, the loud dancehall music booming from the radio at the shops began to fade and we trekked in silence.

It had just rained, and we had to carefully hop over stones in the middle of a small river surrounded by huge eucalyptus trees. I tried to tell Junior the history of the place as it has been told to me over countless trips during the school holidays by my father, and his father, and all my paternal relatives. This was the river they swam in as children. There was the field where my grandfather's cattle grazed, herded by my father and uncles. Here was the shortcut they took to school. Here was the clump of banana trees my aunt hid from the Rhodesian soldiers during the war.

We passed the homesteads of even more relatives whose eyes all slid curiously to Junior; there was something unnervingly magnetic about him and I'd always been quietly jealous of it. I was surly and silent, and always passed everyone's attention or drew it negatively. He was the type of person everyone just couldn't help but look at. In his broken Shona, he told each one of them how wonderful it was to meet them, and each face reflected the same puzzlement. But he was kind enough and they did not take offence. Broken Shona was usually only forgiven in children with excuses to be made for them by parents who had been neglectful enough to not teach them the tongue.

Finally, we reached the tough part of the climb, grunting and heaving until we stood in front of my grandparents' home. Not for the first time,

I wondered if I was doing the right thing by bringing him there. I was fiercely in love with him, and even though there had been no proposal yet, I knew I would marry him.

The reason we had come all this way crashed into me like a powerful wave. My grandmother was dying. I had brought Junior so that even though she would never see my wedding, she would at least see the man I would marry before she died.

The homestead consisted of five buildings: the main house, which we just called House, was the largest of them, painted white, with four rooms, sitting majestically on an incline so you had to turn your head up to look at it. The kitchen, a round little thatched hut recently painted sunshine yellow, lay just a few meters across from the house and next to, on one side, sat a shabby little building with two rooms, and on the other, a small coop which housed the chickens. Behind the kitchen was another hut, which operated mostly as a storage room.

From there, the view was marvellous. The store was a small pinprick in the distance and the valley lay low beneath us, green and dazzling.

Inside the House, we found my grandmother seated quietly in a giant wooden rocking chair, slowly teetering back and forth. She had become small with age and her back was now permanently hunched over. Her heavily wrinkled brown skin, which like mine, had an undertone of red to it, like the earth in the valley, was saggy and hung loose from her bones. It struck me suddenly that she was ninety-three, and ancient. Her hair was thin but still long and floated around her head in silvery wisps like a halo. I turned away from her and took in my surroundings; the living room hadn't changed much in the years since I had been there, the old, checkered beige and yellow sofas were still in the same positions, the heavy teak table was still behind the door, and the gigantic radio that doubled as a record player still sat in the same corner.

Junior waited politely behind me, and I felt him trying to take my hand in his. I smacked it away; public displays of affection were a distinctly European thing, and I wasn't trying to send my frail grandmother early to her grave from shock.

"You keep blocking the light, are you going to stand there and stare at me forever?"

We rushed inside, placing the groceries on the table, next to our luggage that had already been dropped off. We greeted my grandmother in the customary way, hands cupped together and clapping. When I introduced Junior, I told her truthfully what he was to me, and she gave him a once over with her almost milky eyes. I hoped that she approved of him.

"What language do you speak?" she asked him.

"Mainly English." From then on, she made it a point not to speak to him in English.

The sun set and I left for the kitchen to prepare dinner. Junior tried to follow but Grandmama refused, patting the couch next to her and telling him to sit down so they could get to know each other better. I already knew she had many questions for him.

The smoke from the fire in the kitchen choked me, and I frequently had to sit by the door to feel the cool breeze against my face. After dinner, grandmother asked us pointedly what our choice of sleeping arrangements would be, she was too old to care whether we slept together or not and wanted to save us the trouble of sneaking into each other's rooms in the middle of the night. We shared the little room across from hers and tumbled tiredly onto the thin mattress, reaching across for each other. In the dim candlelight, I saw him smile. His teeth, which were almost straight but had little gaps in them, flashed in the dim candlelight. I knew he was happy to be there and wanted to see more of the place in the morning.

Taking him there had been like exposing some part of myself that was even more vulnerable than nakedness. Everything that I was, I was because of that place. He was raised so differently from me, he who had only been to his rural home once, as a baby. I had been to mine nearly every year since I was born. I hoped that by taking him there, I was extending some connection to him that he had never gotten to have.

***

The next morning, Junior was excitedly whisked away by the village boys, Donny and Tadiwa, who had promised to take him herding with them. I envied him his innocence.

Grandmother and I sat on the woven grass mat on the veranda, watching the tiny cars at the tarred road in the distance go left, to Nyanga and beyond, and right, to Mutare.

"Why did you bring him?"

"I want to marry him," I said. "I want you to at least know who I'm going to marry."

She laughed quietly. "He won't marry you."

I was taken aback by the surety in her gravelly voice. A large part of me wanted to dismiss this as the ramblings of a senile old woman who was about to die, taken by the jaws of heart disease, but I knew that wasn't true. Inside me, from the very beginning, existed the gnawing anxiety that one day he would leave me.

"What do you mean he won't marry me?"

She began to stroke my hair with her gnarled hands, like she did when I was a child, parting my hair into sections then pulling it into intricate braids. I was surprised and humiliated to feel tears on my cheeks.

"He is too soft, like fish that breaks apart in a poorly heated pan. He's not ready."

"Then I will wait for him until he is ready."

"Chipo changu," she said. My gift. "He will never be ready." I broke.

The wind blew the wind chimes that hung from the rafters, and they let out a soft tinkle. I lay in her lap, breathing in the scent of the quilt wrapped around her; it smelled like the hearth, like warmth.

I saw Junior on the path that led to the kraal now, next to the garden. His form slowly retreated into the distance, and for a moment, I watched him, lanky but surefooted, the handmade slingshot lent to him by Donny hanging from his hand. I was astonished and ashamed still by how he caught my breath. He was beautiful. He walked with a carefree stride, and painfully I thought, this is how he will come to walk away from me. This was how he would leave me: like the most brilliant sunset, going out in a blaze of glory, without a backward glance in my direction, while I looked on after him for the rest of my life.

"What if one day he is ready? What if I want to wait for him until then?"

She let out a breath, and I could feel the gentle rise and fall of her chest behind me. I could feel the slow and steady thump of her dying heart.

"Then you will waste away your years. You will watch him longingly every day, seeing him love everything and everyone but you with his entire being. Each day you will get up and think, 'Today is different,' but it will be the same until you die. There's a person who he's becoming, and that person cannot love you."

A chasm opened itself up in my chest, and I ached to fill it up with him until I felt whole again. Oh Junior, I thought to myself, how I love you. How I have prostrated myself before you, exalted you like a king, worshipped you like a god. Gladly I would have served in your temple all the days of my life. I would have happily continued to cut off pieces of myself to sacrifice at your altar until there was nothing left.

I couldn't help it now; the tears were streaming steadily down my cheeks, hot and furious, stinging my eyes. I was sobbing into her quilt, mourning everything that I would come to lose: my grandmother, who had loved and protected me since I was a child, and Junior, weak-willed, care-free Junior. The love of my life.

"You are a good girl. I know you brought him here because he has never had this. You want to complete him. You want to help him find those parts of himself that are missing. He doesn't see what you have done for him now, but one day he will understand." She pauses then sighs deeply. "Even when you were a child, all you wanted to do was help people. I think maybe sometimes you do it at the expense of yourself."

Somewhere in the distance, sheep bleated, and cows bellowed mournfully. Her eyes gazed almost unseeingly into that distance.

"There was a man I loved once. I would have set the world on fire to make him warm."

"Did you marry him?" I asked breathlessly.

Wistfully, she sighed. I could feel the nostalgia coming off her in powerful waves. "No. He married someone else, and I married your grandfather. They both died, one after the other in the war, but look child, I am here, many years later, barely alive, but content. Love doesn't always beget happiness. It begets sorrow, separation… heartache; it's not always ours to have. She is an elusive bird. You catch her once, and you stroke her beautiful feathers, pluck one out, and off she flies again. You remain with the feather, to remind you of what you once had."

I realised then that maybe Junior was not the only one who was there to find something within himself. The kraal caught my eye in the distance. I thought of how many times I had come to this place, unaware of his existence, a fat cheeked little girl who barricaded herself in the kitchen hut, terrified to death after the cows had escaped the kraal and were wandering around the homestead. A sullen teenager, perched on the balancing rock that had a clear view of the entire valley and the mountains, hiding away from the rest of the family. There was a life before him, surely there would be one after.

Again, the shocking reality that in not even a year, I would be back again in that place, watching Grandmama's body get lowered into the soil in the family graveyard at the top of the mountain, hit me.

With the curiosity of a child I asked, "Are you afraid to die?" I felt her chest shake behind me with laughter.

"Girl, all my friends are dead. My mother is dead, and my father is dead, and my husband is dead. I have seen all my children become fine adults and seen their children become fine adults. I have kissed great grandchildren and watched this place change with time. I have played my part here. What do I have to fear from death? It is no enemy to me."

I thought about what she said quietly.

"Do you think your boyfriend can stomach slaughtering a goat? I'm in the mood for a goat stew," she said pensively, glancing at the brown goat that grazed on a patch near us, tethered to an orange tree. It began to edge away slowly as if it knew its misfortune.

I laughed. Junior couldn't even kill spiders with a shoe. He overflowed, in some way, with innocence. She mumbled something under her breath that sounded distinctly like "making all this fuss over a man who can't even slaughter us a goat."

"Get Anna and the girls to help you do it then."

I found Anna, another relative and Grandmama's house help, by the cluster of large rocks near the outhouse, bathing her baby. During my early years, my mother would wash me on the flattest of the rocks that was surrounded by green grass and wildflowers, while the sun shone warmly down on us. I would lie on the smooth surface of the rock afterwards, while she washed my clothes, soaking up its warmth, before she would slather my little body in Vaseline, and I would run off to join my cousins to get dirty all over again. Behind the outhouse was a thin, well-worn path that took us to a well and a small pond my mother told me mermaids lived in, which is where we found the rest of the girls, and the path carried on, to Osbourne Dam and beyond.

The business of slaughtering the goat was messy, and Junior squealed and looked queasy when Anna ran the sharp blade of the knife quickly across its neck; it was a merciful death.

***

Later, Junior and I sat perched on a large rock, a cool breeze gently caressing our faces, silently shucking corn. His body was turned toward me, and our knees brushed against each other when I leaned forward to toss the maize husks into an old, battered dish. I found myself suddenly overcome by a random wave of desperation.

"Do you think you'll remember me?" I asked.

"Why wouldn't I?"

Junior laughed a little, tossing a maize husk playfully at my shoulder.

"I'm serious." I clutched at his shirt imploringly and continued. "I want you to never forget me. Please. I want to know that I mattered to you. I want to know that I meant something."

The air was electric with a sense of urgency. I could feel bile rising in the back of my throat. This was fear. Fear of losing him, but even worse, much worse, the fear of being forgotten.

Junior placed both my hands in his; they were less calloused, more delicate than mine. I liked to entertain the idea that he made me a softer woman than I was by nature. I liked to believe that he made me gentle. He held me like this for a while, our hands clasped firmly together. I felt utterly consumed by my love for him. Please, I wanted to say. Please don't leave me.

"You are the love of my life. I could never forget you. Of course I'll remember you, and I'll remember this," he said, gesturing animatedly to our environment.

He stared at me intently, and we clutched each other like people possessed. I look back on those moments and realise that was love in its climax, love fighting for its last dying breaths. Love battling for survival. I had the distinct and acute feeling somewhere inside me that I would never see him again. Some kind of anticipatory grief perhaps, and a helplessness from the knowledge that there was nothing I could do about it. Years passed after we left that place, time running continuous laps, and I never saw him since. I found that no matter how hard I tried, I could never forget that brief summer holiday with Junior. The memory of him, the memory of that place, stayed stubbornly in me old, obstinate stain. I have felt the pain of his depart nearly every day since.

Clouds had begun to gather in large imposing sky. There was a distant clap of thunder.

"Maybe we should go," Junior said, pulling

He looked back at me then, really looked at me, and saw in his eyes a certain unbridgeable distance that had begun to form between us. Extending an arm to me, he gazed at me intensely while our arms locked as he pulled me up and said, "Nothing about you could ever be forgettable."

***

On the last day, Grandmama called us both to her. Her warm and rough hands grasped the sides of my face and she whispered, "He's a fool for failing to truly value you, but don't join him in his foolishness by also failing to value yourself."

I hated that I wept so easily; she was wiping away my stinging salty tears with her thumbs. There would be no next time. When I saw her again, she would be a body, lowered into the red soil in the graveyard higher up the mountain that looked over the whole district. Her grave would be beside my grandfather's, and behind hers, the grave of a sister who died when we were children.

"You know what we believe, don't forget it," she said. To my people, those that still called on midzimu, death was not the end but merely a door to the next world. She would join the long line of my ancestors, who are my guardians in this life until I can join them in the next. "I'll always be there."

From my peripheral vision, I saw Junior standing awkwardly in the corner, trying his best to be invisible, which was ridiculous considering how much of an attention magnet he was. He could never be invisible.

"And you, come here." He jolted, surprised to be addressed at all, and nearly tripped over himself rushing to her side. Grandmama regarded him seriously in silence for a minute. A week of country air had done him well, and his radiance almost made me want to look away. His skin shone like it had been dipped in the purest honey. There was something different about his aura then. Before, he had been like a tree with shallow roots, disconnected from his heritage, a pale shadow of the white man. Now, that internal missing piece of the puzzle that was his identity was beginning to be shaped.

Grandmama also put her hands, calloused from decades of labour, on the sides of his face. Hands that had caught babies escaping the wombs of their mothers, and hands that had held the dying bodies of her children.

"Much has been taken from us" she said, "Do not let your identity be taken from you also."

She placed each one of her hands in one of ours and called upon her gods to give us blessings. Outside, I took a last glimpse of my rural home, how I wanted to remember it. Vhumbunu sprawled beneath me, all green trees; tall gumtrees spread along the line of the thin stream, dense Msasas in the wood, little huts and kraals and the Methodist church by the shops; the grapevine around the dara and the Mazhanje trees; Uncle Jaire's homestead below us, where Donny and Tadiwa lived; the mountains, high and powerful all around, the peaks, which were once holy and revered to my people, blue and shrouded in white mist. They were said to be where the spirits reside. I remembered my father teaching my sisters and I to point at them with our fists and not our index fingers, to show our respect. A gentle cool breeze was tender against my cheek. The earth, red and brown, and fertile with maize and sugarcane that grew tall out of it, and tea that sprawled along the ground. Grandmama's House, a faded white, and Grandmama, bright and wise, seated on the carved wooden chair on the grey polished veranda, looked down into the valley.

Gift Mukunga

Gift Mukunga lives in Bulawayo, Zimbabwe. He is married with two boys in their early twenties. He is an accountant by profession but has always loved writing. In primary school, he had a story published by the Ministry of Education. When he was in Form 4, he was one of the winners of the Randalls Essay Competition. Since then, he did not write anything of note until 2020, when he had a story included in an anthology published by Intwasa.

X (formerly Twitter): @giviemurehwa
Facebook: Gift Mukunga

A Death In The Morning
Gift Mukunga – Zimbabwe

I was roused from my slumber with a start. Something wasn't right. I dragged open the ill-fitting door of the hut. The jagged bottom, with a grating sound that put my teeth on edge, made neat quarter circle grooves in the mud floor. I stooped low to avoid the unkempt thatch hanging over the door as I stepped out into the tepid morning sunlight. The birdsong that I usually woke up to had been replaced by the din of angry men's voices shouting over each other. I raised my hand to my brow, squinting a little as my sleepy eyes adjusted to the light. The chill in the morning air was quickly giving way to the warmth of the sun, which was now rising into the cloudless sky, over the endless hills and expansive valleys of Shamva.

My grandfather's homestead was on the side of a gentle hill, with the gravel road, running like a dusty ribbon through the village, just below it. That was the site of the commotion. A number of the villagers had formed a small but raucous crowd around a big, white SUV that was stopped in the middle of the road. The thick coat of dust on it failed to quite hide its shiny newness as the sunbeams bursting through the trees danced on it. I couldn't quite make out what was being said, but a heated confrontation was going on between the village youths and the smartly dressed occupants of the big car who had now disembarked. There was a lot of gesticulating by both sides, first toward the car, and then to the ground, and back to the car... on and on it went. I couldn't see what was on the ground as my sight was obscured by the crowd. Despite being outnumbered, the obviously city folk did not seem at all intimidated, shouting and waving their arms about with equal fervour at the youths, some of whom showed signs of having overindulged in the local brew the previous night.

I cautiously sauntered towards the commotion, trepidation beginning to make my heart beat that much faster, afraid of what I would see on the ground. I pushed my way through the crowd to see what it was. There, in the dust, Majoki lay. His body lay in such an awkward way that it could only mean broken bones. He wasn't dead yet. His big brown eyes blinked slowly, so moist they seemed fluid. There was such a look of calmness in them, like he had accepted his fate and made peace with it. As the life ebbed out of him, he was oblivious to cacophony going on around him.

What broke my heart, even more than the sight of Majoki calmly dying in the dust, was the sight of Takadii kneeling besides him. If there was anything of value that Takadii had in this world, it was Majoki. Takadii had had it tough, having lost both his parents to the ravages of AIDS, back in the days when it was spoken of in hushed tones. In those days, it was easier to say I am bewitched that to say I am HIV positive and get the appropriate treatment. That is how his mother went to her grave, believing that her unmarried cousin was bewitching her so she could take her husband for herself. As if to thwart that possibility, it seemed she called her husband to follow, for it wasn't long before he lay beside her.

So it was that little Takadii became the ward of his frail grandmother. They survived the best they could, but it is safe to say that without the largesse of the other villagers, they would have starved to death. At least his parents had left him with Majoki and November. When Takadii had become a little older, able to hold the plough, they would work their piece of land together. Takadii loved Majoki and November; they were almost like brothers to him. Life had become a little easier. But then November died. It was during the previous rainy season that a mysterious illness had swept through the land, striking many down. November had not been spared. It had been such a blow for Takadii, it was like experiencing the death of his parents again. He had come to terms with it, hoping he would be able to hire another to pair with Majoki this season. But now Majoki was inhaling the dust of the road in shallow breaths, slipping away from this life.

The older man of the trio from the car was going on about the cost of fixing his car. A fair chunk of the front was mangled, and an airbag had deployed. He told the villagers they were very lucky he was insured, otherwise they would have to sell all their cattle to pay for his repairs. There was an uproar of indignation at this slight, although the man wasn't far from the truth. The gulf between their penury and his opulence would require many cattle to bridge. He went on berating the villagers for letting their livestock stray onto the road, whilst they scolded him for speeding recklessly through the village. In the end, the man saw no hope in getting any compensation from the villagers. Besides, this was a minor inconvenience to him. A call to his insurer and a few days in the workshop, his car would be as good as new. So after a little bit more shouting and an exchange of curses, the city folk jumped into their big car, drove around Majoki and sped off in a cloud of dust.

As the car faded into the distance, the dust clouds billowing behind it, the mood amongst the villagers had slowly turned jovial. One of the youths had brought an axe to finally put the injured ox out of its misery. Another had brought knives to skin the ox, and a woman had brought a big dish for the offal. I walked over to Takadii, who was still kneeling beside his beloved ox. I gently pulled him up and walked him away as the axe sunk into the back of Majoki's head. He had a look of utter defeat on his face. The man with the big car had gone, and in a week or so would have forgotten this episode. The villagers would enjoy a bit of meat for a few days. They would pay him for the meat of course, but it would never compensate for his ox. They would talk about this incident for a while, pity him, and then carry on with their lives. He sat down heavily onto the ground a little distance away from the frenzy around Majoki, who was now being meticulously butchered. He hung his head as a man who had lost all he had in the world. I sat next to him, mute. No words I could say would suffice. As the ruckus died down, I could hear the birds again. The sun shone in the azure sky. The verdant hills slowly morphed to blue as they stretched into the distance. Suddenly, the beauty of the day seemed cruel.

***

About a week had passed since the demise of Majoki. Takadii and I sat on the earthen bench that arched along the wall of the round brick hut that was vaSarai, Takadii's grandmother's kitchen. It was late morning, going towards noon, but the sun had remained hidden behind the dark, thick rain clouds. The rain came down in a stiff drizzle, the kind that went on the whole day. The gentle drip-drip of the water rolling off the thatch of the hut, into the containers that vaSarai had put out, made a soothing sound, occasionally punctuated by the croak of a frog or the call of a bird. Wisps of smoke rose from the hearth in the centre of the room, up towards the conical roof. The interior thatch had been blackened by years of such fires, and soot hung in clumps off the ancient cobwebs at the top of the cone, where vaSarai could not reach with her stick. The fire would almost die, then vaSarai would coax it back to life, stoking the embers and blowing on it as hard as her old lungs would allow. We were shelling the last of last season's peanuts and vaSarai would occasionally scold us for eating about as many peanuts as we would put into the *rusero* on the floor. Her tone though, told us she really didn't mind. The conversation was light-hearted, if somewhat subdued. It was almost an idyllic scene, were it not for the smoked remains of Majoki, cut in strips and hung on a string held up by two nails hammered into the mud bricks, to remind everyone of the tragedy that had occurred only a few days ago.

"*Muzukuru…*" vaSarai turned her head towards her grandchild. "Now that the rains are here, we have to prepare the field…" her voice trailed off. Although her head was toward Takadii, she was looking past him, through the doorway, her eyes locked on the small granary that was about ten metres away, directly opposite the kitchen entrance. It was the only square building in the little compound. It was built off the ground, upon a platform of thick logs resting on big boulders. Her chickens had found refuge from the rain beneath it, scratching the ground for what little morsels they could find. Would they be able to fill it again this season?

"*Mbuya…*" Takadii responded to his grandmother, grateful for the lack of eye contact, because the sadness in her eyes was too much for him. Whenever he did look into them, the sadness would pour out of her eyes, and engulf him like icy cold water, seeping through his very soul, into his bones, and bringing into stark relief, his own impotence at changing their situation. "We may not be able to find someone to lend us oxen this year, since many were lost during that illness that took November, but I have spoken to my friends, and they will come to help us work the field by hand. We just have to make sure that there is enough of the brew for them." I wondered which friends he meant since, as far as I was aware, I was the only one. It seemed this was something he had just said to reassure his grandmother. VaSarai seemed to see through the ruse but was reassured by it nonetheless. Still, it was a feasible idea. I knew a number of the village youths would be happy to come and work the field in exchange for beer. VaSarai, unfortunately, had never brewed beer in her life, that possibility having been thwarted by the fact that her father had been one of the most zealous students of the Christian missionaries that had established themselves in the area at the advent of colonialism. Nevertheless, it was a small hurdle. For a chicken or two, one of the other village ladies would brew the beer.

"*Gogogoi…*" a deep, raspy voice, accompanied by clapping hands, startled all of us.

"Come in, come in vaMasembura." VaSarai's invitation was a bit redundant as vaMasembura had already stepped in and we sidled along the bench to make room for him. VaMasembura was the village headman. He had on his trademark blue worksuit and a pair of black gumboots. Come rain or shine, grand occasion or working in the fields, that's what he wore. His scraggly beard and short but unkempt hair were less of a fashion statement and more a case of someone who couldn't be bothered about grooming. His face was etched with deep wrinkles, making him look older than he really was. His appearance was due less to the passage of time and more to the ravages of hard drinking and the hand rolled tobacco he was partial to.

"Is everything alright where you're coming from vaMasembura, for you to come through the rain like this?" vaSarai asked, head slightly tilted, looking at vaMasembura with an expression of one expecting trouble. She didn't have much respect for the headman. He was known to be a devious man, in whose court, justice could be bought with a calabash of beer.

"No, all is well where I have come from, vaSarai. How are things here?" vaMasembura replied. There was more small talk, but it felt like the beginning of a battle. Two boxers circling each other, looking for an opening. Finally, vaMasembura felt he had sized up his opponent enough; it was time to throw the first punch. "So, vaSarai, as you might have heard, Goredema's son is coming back from the city for good. He lost his job because of this disease that keeps us wearing these cloth muzzles. The company closed down," he said, tugging at his facemask that was pulled down to his chin.

VaSarai looked at him quizzically, waiting for him to continue. When he didn't, she spoke. "Yes, I have heard that. But what does it have to do with me?" A hint of irritation came through in her voice, and it seemed to unsettle the headman a little.

"Well, umm… I… I…" The headman stammered, realising he might have more of a fight on his hands than he had bargained for. "Well… he didn't have a homestead. And Goredema has parcelled out all his land to his other sons, he has none left to give him."

"So!?" vaSarai shot back. She was bristling now, venom loaded in that single word.

VaMasembura was now not as sure of himself as when he had walked in. "So… er…" since you have no more oxen, we thought we should cut your field to a size you can man–" He didn't finish his sentence. VaSarai had pulled out a burning log, about the thickness of her thin forearm, from the fire and thrown it as hard as her frail frame would allow at vaMasembura. It didn't quite land on its target but hit the floor with a shower of sparks. Although most of the sparks landed on vaMasembura, some had landed on Takadii and I. All three of us on the bench had jumped up and were now furiously brushing away the tiny little embers on our clothes.

"*Iwe* Masembura! *Usauye kuzondisembura pano*, don't come and provoke me!" vaSarai berated vaMasembura. She addressed him now as she would a little boy, for indeed she remembered seeing him as a snot nosed little toddler many years ago. This was not the first time that vaMasembura had coveted vaSarai's field. Ever since her son, Takadii's father, had died, the headman had been trying to wrestle the field from her. It was known that the headman took money to resettle people illegally in the area. He had not spared even the grazing lands. He obviously greased the right palms in higher offices and thus far had remained untouched by the law. VaSarai's field was prime land that he could make a lot of money from.

"You witch!" vaMasembura hissed at vaSarai, stumbling towards her with his arm raised.

Takadii jumped between his grandmother and the headman and grabbed the raised arm. "Hey old man, what do you think you're doing!?" This was not the timid Takadii I knew. It was like something had snapped inside him. The vehemence with which he shouted at vaMasembura I had not seen before. His other hand was now grabbing vaMasembura's collar and he was pushing him out of the door with a strength that belied his gaunt, undernourished body.

"Boy, you think you're grown now, hey? Let me go right now…" the headman squawked, his legs flailing, desperately trying to keep his balance. VaMasembura's heel caught on the raised threshold, and he tumbled over backwards into the rain, taking Takadii with him. Takadii immediately scrambled to his feet and would have stomped on vaMasembura had I not rushed out to hold him back.

VaMasembura was feebly trying to get up from the mud and shouting at the same time. "Your grandmother is a witch! She ate her own children, she will eat you too! Look how thin you are, she is eating you already!" Takadii swung his foot hard, but I tugged him back, and it narrowly missed the headman's head. "You will regret boy, I am going to take that field. You will see…" his voice trailed off, like he wasn't convinced of what he was saying. Takadii must have sensed this because I felt his body relax. I let him go. He stood over vaMasembura like a mighty warrior over a vanquished foe. VaMasembura was now on all fours but just couldn't get himself to stand as he kept slipping in the mud. Takadii grabbed him by the back of his collar and pulled him up. After getting steady on his feet, the headman shook Takadii's hand off and started plodding through the puddles, out of vaSarai's compound.

All this while, Takadii's grandmother, who was now standing in the doorway of her kitchen, had been shouting for the headman to leave her compound and never come back. Now that he was leaving, she turned her attention to her grandson. She looked at him with pride. She had always worried whether he would be able to look after himself, stand up for himself when she was gone. He had always been timid and allowed others to take advantage of him. But she had seen a transformation in that moment he grabbed the headman to protect her. A fire had awoken within him. And she could see that he himself had realised the strength within him. VaMasembura may try again, but now that mountain had turned into a molehill. If she were to die today, she would die happy, knowing that yes, the boy had grown and was willing to fight for what was his.

Joseph Jegede

Joseph Jegede hails from Ondo state in Nigeria. He graduated with first-class honours from Obafemi Awolowo University, Nigeria. He is also an alumnus of Ludwig Maximillian University of Munich, Germany, where he attended the summer school after he was awarded a scholarship by the DAAD in 2021. As a thinker and interested observer of social affairs and human nature, Joseph Jegede expresses himself by writing fictional stories. His works have been longlisted and shortlisted for the Awele Creative Trust Prize and Kepress Anthology prize respectively. His works have further appeared in Hotpot Magazine, The Kalahari Review, Novelty Fiction Gazette and elsewhere. He is passionate about freedom of expression. He loves playing on words.

Things You Cannot Say With Your Mouth
Joseph Jegede – Nigeria

Come out of hiding, you're safe here with me.

***

If you were to measure the size of your penis with your mother's tape rule, it should be about twelve inches long. Your balls hang loosely in their bag as you observe the gradual rising of your third leg. It is now twice its shrunken size, and the sight of it reminds you of the rising of dough. As you glance at the phone which you hold in your left hand, you stroke gently at first, with your right hand, until it takes you to the sixth heaven. After thirteen strokes, you cum, and the favours shoot out, splashing all over your bare tummy, extending to your chest, and almost reaching your face. Apart from the fact that it allows breezes to reach your balls, this is one other reason why you enjoy staying indoors unclad. You pause the video and let the phone drop on the mattress. Ensuring the milky white substance is not wasted, you begin to spoon it with your fingers which you rub onto your face afterward. Your pimples should disappear soon. You rub the rest of the cum around your body till the thick liquid screams *auf Wiedersehen,* and all you can see are streaks and patterns. And then you heave and rest your eyes on the 6×6 ceiling of your room as if the asbestos have never been there. You stare down at your weapon-of-massive-destruction again and see it has shrunken like withered *ugwu* leaves. And there in your eyes is a longing, a want for the real thing. For ecstasy.

***

Your mother says social media will be the end of you. You consider it equal to the probability of you dying of a panic attack at 1:00 am like your father, which is sixty percent. Right now, you scroll through Twitter, prying into the things people say about themselves; their reservations about their friends and families; their general opinion of the world, and of course, what kind of life they expect from public figures. You drop comments under some posts while you just scroll past others. Next time, when your mother tells you social media could ruin you, tell her how from the corners of your room you can receive live reports of the earthquake in Turkey, of the assaults on voters in Nigeria, and even of how it enables you to participate in the *#endsars* and *#justiceformohbad* protests from the corners of your room. Tell her also how it broadens your horizon and helps you learn new things like the new word you just learned: bigotry.

As you scroll through the feeds, you stumble on a post by the BBC stating that women in Berlin may now swim topless in pools. You tarry a while on that post before scrolling past it. There is a traffic of thoughts in your mind that could trigger a panic attack if you read further. Yet you continue. Afterall, do you not derive pleasure from the risky things of life? The painful *risky* kind that you often describe as *sweet pain*? When at night you lay down and sleep, you think of the world, and of what it's becoming, of the small things that are said and the big things that are often left unsaid, of the painful and the pleasurable. And because the only thing you fear more than a panic attack in the middle of the night is wanting to defecate while in transit in a public bus, you bottle your thoughts and go to bed. And when you sleep, the thing between your legs begins to fight you.

***

You go to church today. The one close to your hostel. Although it's been a long time since you last attended one, you are still familiar with the Pentecostal routine. Just that here, today, there is an inclusion of a children's presentation before the pastor's message. You watch as the children file out in a straight line towards the altar like roaches, arranging themselves according to their *gogolarity* – like your mother would say when describing people who lined up according to their heights. They are presenting a song, and you admire the innocence with which they execute the task. Their lead vocalist, a boy of about ten, slim with dark skin like camwood, recites some bible verses next. It earns him cheers from the congregation, except you. The boy reminds you of something: his gesture, the sharpness of his speech, the rolling of his eyes, and even his steps as he catwalks about the altar. You would love to see his parents

190

and observe their response to this child. So when the announcer announced afterward that first-timers should come out for recognition, you don't, even though you would have loved to get that chilled coke and Digestive *biscuits* they give to first-timers. On one hand, you must get out of this crowded place and return to your solitude, on the other, you must observe that child after service. However, when service ends, you do not see him or any of the other kids who presented with him. So you step out of the church premises onto the road leading home and let the sun laugh at your foolishness as you walk the few distances back to your house. And as you walk, the thought of that boy accompanies you as you ask yourself whether he will always be like that. But even you know that is not up for debate.

***

You are going through Twitter when you stumble upon a tweet that says Ugandan lawmakers have passed a bill into law criminalising homosexuality, making it punishable with ten years imprisonment. As if by impulse, you spring up from the mattress where you lay all day, close the windows, and put on the standing fan, then you face the mirror and begin to mumble your thoughts to the man in the mirror. "No society should be in a position to dictate to individuals what they should do with their body." Because you see the interest on the man's face, you continue. "Yes, to criminalise a person's sexual preference is to criminalise their identity. It tramples upon their human rights. Besides, there are more problems that need to be solved in these extremist African countries than getting concerned with men who kiss men and women who kiss women. What the fuck! Like what the actual heck…" and then you hear a bang on your door. It is intense. It is then you stop and realise that you have *poomsaed* away from the mirror and have broken your favourite ceramic plate, scattered your books, and destroyed your newly bought Bluetooth speaker. You sink into the mattress and choose to ignore the untidiness of the room. Instead, you pick up your phone again and continue on Twitter like a wife going back to her abusive husband. You scroll through a series of tweets before you come across a video that interests you. The five second video shows two slim figures, both light-skinned with dark knuckles, wearing bone-straight hairs and crop tops on skinny jeans. One can easily see through the effort they employ in showing and shaking their small *bumbums* for the camera as they chew gum like bad bitches in their high heeled shoes. While their heavily painted faces could fool one into thinking their menstrual cycles are around the corner, their flat chests give away that their penises are probably as huge as yours. Perhaps they should have worn padded bras, you think. Yet it causes you to ponder the news which you read earlier and wonder whether you had been right in criticising those governments. But that in itself is the irony of life: sometimes we become the exact people we hate. So you leave Twitter and go to the vault where you keep things other eyes must not see, click on a video, and begin to watch. You can feel the sensation in your groin as your eyes dance to the display on your screen. Your hands move and begin to stroke the wood above your two sagging balloons. After fifteen strokes, you release. And deep down, somewhere down your gut, there remains that insatiable hunger. After you have cleaned up with a napkin which you now keep by your side for that purpose, you look at the upheaved state of your room and ask yourself what day it is. You count from Monday and realise it is *eti*. Fridays are never good for you.

***

Earlier today, when you had a WhatsApp group call with your friends, they talked about going to New Buka later in the evening. They asked if you would be coming, and because you knew it was pointless telling them you had assignments to submit, or presentations to prepare for etc., you said yes. School was on break, after all. But after the call, you smiled to yourself because you knew that just like the *P* in *Psalms*, their expectations would be futile. So when you hear a bang on your door later in the evening it startles you, even though the gesture seems so familiar. You hurry and dump the plate you used to eat beans earlier into the sink, before flinging the clothes sitting on the mattress into the wardrobe. Then you throw yourself into a pair of shorts that fail to hide your dickprint, and a sleeveless top, spray some air freshener in the room and perfume on your body before opening the door to Deola.

"Foolish boy, shey it's me that's making you to go through all this ceremony, as if pe I've not seen your worst," she says, as she pushes her tall slim frame through the door and settles into your bed before you can comment on her fitting crop top and boyfriend jeans trousers which make her look like the model she is. You smile instead.

"Why you no tell me say you dey come?" You ask.

"Because if I had told you, you would have given one silly excuse pe you no dey house. Abi I lie?" She says, looking into your eyes. You smile, knowing full well she is right.

"So, young man, go and get dressed let's start going." She says.

"Okay, oya, you don catch me. But honestly I have a meeting by seven, I need to submit a task today too and I've not done it, I must…"

"Young man, e yaff do. I'm used to that. Go and get dressed, the others are waiting for us at the club. We won't be long. Do fast."

You bow to pressure and enter the bathroom. You are set for the outing after multiple attempts by Deola to help you find suitable wear.

***

And there at the club in New Buka, with the dramatic lighting which changes the colour of your white t-shirt to the colour purple and sometimes to red or green, you watch as your friends drink and gossip. They tell you to order Desperado; it doesn't contain much alcohol. But when you put the drink in your mouth, its smell almost causes you to puke. You leave it and wander your eyes around the club, looking at people drinking in companies at strategic corners of the clubhouse. Through the entrance, men walk in with women you assume to be their partners. And then *he* walks in, his tall and stout frame sounding an alarm. Even in the dramatic light, you can still make out his light skin. He used to be your senior and you never liked him because you thought he was too *razz*. He sits with you guys and tells you to order anything you want. So this time you request Chivita and they bring you the big one. You drink in silence while Deola and the rest of your friends are lost in their drunken conversation about movies. What a good way to sideline someone who detests TVs? Out of frustration, you take a very large gulp of the fruit juice, and by the time you take a break and look up, you catch the senior staring at you as smoke from his weed escapes through his mouth and nostrils. You've always liked the smell of smoke despite not being a smoker. You only hold his gaze for a while before breaking away from it and begin to press your phone. You cannot wait to get out of here.

And then out of the blues, he says, "You are in your final year now, I guess." You nod and he continues over the loud music playing in the background. "Hope you are preparing yourself for the life out there." You stare at him because you don't know what to say. You eventually tell him the thought of life after school scares you often. So he stands from his seat opposite you and comes to sit in the space beside you, just spacious enough to contain his small butt. He begins to show you pictures from his phone, some of which cause you to swallow hard, as he simultaneously gives you words of encouragement.

"You need to be prepared for life out there. Look at me for instance, I did history, but ended up working in HR…" The rest of the things he says do not stick to your mind as your eyes are lost in the movement of his lips and the bulginess of his once flat cheeks. And then he says, "William Blake says 'make your own rules or be a slave to another man's.'" You don't know how you got here, but you nod. And then he gives you his number and says you should write him on WhatsApp. You nod as you wonder whether his presence here today was planned or just a mere coincidence. And when your drunk friends begin to drag their shaky feet out of the club, you tarry before trailing behind them, wishing they would stay longer.

***

It is late when you get back home. You freshen up and remain unclad as you prepare to go to bed. As you scroll through Twitter to be kept abreast of what you have missed during the day, your senior's face clouds your mind and a smile creeps in. Out of the blue, the thing between your legs begins to combat you, chokes you, pins you to the ground even. You yield as you exit Twitter, drop your phone by your side and begin to stroke. You remember the movement of his lips, the way the smoke emitted through his mouth and nostrils, the hoarseness of his voice, and the coarseness of his palms when he first shook your hand. You close your eyes and smile, and soon you feel your body shuddering and about to explode. You don't mind a panic attack right now. A moan, more like a false falsetto than a terrible treble, escapes from your throat as you feel

194

warm splashes all over your belly. This time around, you do not reach for the napkin by your bedside to clean up, or hurry to the bathroom. You have no idea how many strokes either. You must own this feeling. Gradually, your eyes begin to close in sleep as your face smiles in deep ecstasy.

www.ingramcontent.com/pod-product-compliance
Lightning Source LLC
Chambersburg PA
CBHW011559190726
48287CB00010B/2969